CATALOG OF DESIRE AND DISAPPEARANCE

ANA CRUZ

CATALOG OF DESIRE AND DISAPPEARANCE

ISBN: 9798391955344

CONTENTS

1: ART AND HISTORY

Ana Wolf headed home on the deserted streets of Lichtenberg, Berlin, wearing skinny black trousers tucked sloppily into the collar of her lackluster leather boots. She loosely secured the tips of her curly, tousled auburn hair with an antic scrunchy that matched the beige lapels of her red boucle coat.

The May air smelled of newly cut grass and freshly baked muffins. The blend of the aromas triggered a familiar dopamine rush. She knew that Flora, her grandmother, would have set the dinner table with homemade bread and a foreign, sour sauce in anticipation of her arrival. Ana looked forward to the burst of flavor in her mouth, followed by a warm, deserving bath, then she could relax in bed with the novel she took home from work.

Ana worked in the Lichtenberg public library where it was her job to pick up after cocky bibliophiles, who did not bother to return the hardbacks to the shelf nor leave the library seats the way they met them. But amidst the hushing of rows of excited teenagers, who only came to check fashion magazines and marvel at entries in the *Guinness Book of World Records* and peeling chewed gum off from under the library tables and chairs, Ana actually loved her job.

She was able to steal away to the back room with her favorite books in hand whenever her coworker was at the front desk, handling the library visitors. As an art historian, she consumed Giorgio Vasari's publication of famed artists' biographies, *Lives of the Most Excellent Painters, Sculptors, and Architects*. When she was not reading about celebrated artists, it was about their art. That evening, she snuck Dan Brown's *Inferno* into the middle zip of her laptop bag. One thing she enjoyed about being a library worker was that she got to take and return books as she pleased without filling out the records. In two days, she would be done with the novel and maybe return for something more muliebral like the works of Leonardo da Vinci.

She got to the big brown door of her childhood home. Her parents were still very much in the picture, but being enterprising entrepreneurs all her life, they had given up most of their parental roles to Ana's paternal grandmother. When she saw the Audi parked at the fore of the house, Ana braced herself for whatever impact seeing her parents would bring.

"Oh, honey. You're home?" Her mother, Anne, waltzed through the spacious corridor to give her daughter a hug.

"You didn't tell me you'd be back today."

"Really?" Anne turned to look at her husband, who was Ana's father and Flora's son. "I did. She must have missed it."

Ana was just beginning to shake her head when her mother pulled the coat off her shoulders and hung it on the coat hanger, ushering her into the kitchen where Flora was just bringing bread out of the oven. Anne continued, "Flora said she found this recipe online and tried to cook it. It's her first attempt, but we are sure it will be delicious."

Ana wanted to tell her mom that she joined Flora in searching for the recipe online and decided it was not a bad idea to attempt. They bought the ingredients together, but you couldn't really blame a woman for wanting to exercise supremacy in her home, as if the decision and the permission for Flora to experiment with a foreign meal were given by her. After all, she was Mrs. Wolf, co-founder of the Wolf Fashion Empire.

"Smells good, Mamma," Ana's father said to Flora and put his arms around his mother. She wiggled it off with the satisfied grin of an appreciated mother. Then, she motioned for Ana to help her with the cooling racks.

"Dinner will be set in ten minutes."

Anne made her way out of the kitchen, seeing that her help was not needed. Not that it was ever needed in culinary matters. Ana learned everything she knew about cooking from Flora, but Anne had no interest in cooking; it was beneath her. Although they shared the same red hair color and the same curvy, slender figure, Ana's mores were nothing like her mother's grandiose lifestyle.

Ana watched her mother swing her hips out of the kitchen. She knew it would not be long before her mother returned with another purport intended to reinstate her authority as the woman of the home.

The bread had cooled, and dinner was set. The evening was not going as Ana had planned it. Her abandoned novel stayed hidden from any rays of light between papers and a laptop in the oxblood bag. Her father sat down heavily at the head of the table while his graceful wife took her position by his left side. Ana was opposite her mother, and Flora took her seat by her granddaughter. They said a prayer and dug in.

Ana tore off a piece of the freshly baked bread and dipped it into the sauce while ignoring Anne, who toyed noisily with her cutlery and the food on her plate. Anne had packed her long, curly hair into a neat ponytail, away from her eyes and face, while Ana blew a tuft of hair from her eyes and stuffed her mouth with bread.

"So, Ana," Anne leaned towards the table, "Any guy yet?" She faked a giggle like she and Ana were girlfriends who talked about their crushes at secondary school weeknight parties.

Ana furrowed her eyebrows and pursed her thin lips.

Her mother stared back and then gradually made her face into that of shock, complete with wide eyes, raised brows, and open mouth that was only decently concealed by manicured fingers. She swung her gaze and fastened it on her husband. "She's still single... after all this time."

The taste of sour cream in Ana's mouth began to burn, but she could not chew nor swallow.

Her father reached across the table and took her hand, which was still holding a large piece of bread. "Your mother and I were talking. There is no easy way to say this but—"

"We think you're old enough to move out," interrupted Anne.

Ana managed to chew and swallow. She always knew this day would come, but it was less of a demurral than she thought it would be. "That's not an issue at all. I will start looking for flats tomorrow."

"Yes, but we will not let you move out to live on your own," said Anne, "You should be married first."

Ana coughed out her bread. Flora quickly handed her a glass of water. Anne was still talking, oblivious that her daughter almost choked. "You see, young girls these days just leave their parents' houses and do whatever they like. They go ahead and live with men they are not married to or spend nights in dangerous places. We don't want that for you."

"I think you should start taking dating seriously now. Find Mr. Right," her dad said.

Ana could feel sweat breaking out from her pores. Flora might have felt it, too, because she was now shifting uneasily on her chair.

"We are not kicking you out. We are just urging you to put yourself out there and let people know that you are on the market."

Ana scoffed at how her father did not know that his choice of words offended her as her mother shoved a phone into her face. "I heard that these dating apps are what young people like you use these days. Have you heard of PairMeUp?" The app had a logo of a cartoon couple holding hands and smiling from ear to ear. Ana thought it looked childish.

"I believe Ana would like to do it the old-fashion way." Again, Flora came to the rescue.

Anne shrugged. "Anyhow, we are just asking that you're dating the next time we come back."

"Which is?"

"After the fashion week in Milan. We will be here for a few days till we fly out to the city of art and culture, so you have at least two weeks."

Ana loved Italy but somehow felt upset hearing it mentioned in this way. Dinner was eaten in silence from that moment till the table was cleared, at least for those who could still eat. The schnitzel in hollandaise sauce and baked potatoes lost all taste to Ana. Even the thought of the unfinished novel in her bag was not calming enough. The whole night had been spoiled, and hopefully, she would be in a good mood at work the next day.

Andre was dropping the day's papers on the newspaper rack and clearing away older ones when Ana walked into the library. "Well, hello there." His greeting was not complete without hand gestures and a very welcoming smile. Andre was her coworker and the closest thing to a best friend she had. They both shared the same thoughts and feelings towards their job and the people who walked in every day. They got along well.

"Hey, Andre."

"Oh no. I'm picking up something in your voice. What's wrong?" He blinked excessively and pouted his full lips, bringing his palms together at chin level. Andre's eyes followed Ana to where she dropped her sleek laptop bag on her chair. She pulled out the Dan Brown novel and flung it onto the table.

"Rough night. I didn't get to read that."

"Are your parents back?" he heaved.

Ana did not need to reply.

"Oh no." His hands were in his kinky black hair. Andre was the stereotypical example of a man who cared way too much about their hair, skin, and clothes. He was a gallant gentleman like her father, but unlike her father, Andre was gay. "What are they on to now."

"They want me to get a boyfriend." Ana dropped her hands in sheer frustration. She was expecting some kind of sympathy from her coworker, but his plump lips spread apart as he broke into a snicker.

"Not helping, Andre."

"Okay, sorry. But how are you going to do that?" he said in a deep and melodic sing-song voice.

"I don't know." She threw herself into her seat and fumbled with the tangles in her hair.

"I can help with that."

"Don't touch my hair."

"I wasn't talking about that," he rolled his eyeballs back into their sockets. "I can help you get a guy. I know one who is as desperate as you."

Ana blew a few strands of hair from her eyes.

"I thought you'd be more excited."

"Well, I'm not desperate."

"Girl, you're twenty-eight going on forty. You should be."

Andre returned to his job at the newspaper stand while Ana tried to find her place in the novel. She checked the records, arranged the seats, and verified that all books were placed appropriately on their shelves the day before just so that she could have more time with her book in the morning. Ana could hardly concentrate on the words on the page even though she was at a very exciting part. She closed the book.

"So, you said you know someone. You know my fears already."

Andre arched the eyebrow on the same side of his face as his smirk. "Glad you're interested. Trust me, he doesn't care about all that. He is just like you."

"Wait, what?"

"I mean, he's into art and stuff like that, not necessarily that he doesn't comb his hair or wears the same shoes every day.

"Hey, they're sturdy, and they still fit."

He shrugged.

"So, he won't care that I'm not like other girls?"

"I think he will be willing to overlook that, Ana," Andre said assuredly.

Ana picked up her book again but slapped it back on the table. "Can I see a photo?"

"Don't have one."

"Where do you know him from."

"He's a friend of my brother's. Actually, his tutor."

"What course?"

"Something about sexing and canvas—art and gender. Oh, and he was the one that helped my bro pass his modern and contemporary art and design class." Andre heard Ana gasp. "I told you he was into your kind of shit."

"And you're sure he won't mind my messiness?"

"I'm positive, Ana."

They eased into their work. Ana could now find time to focus on the novel in between helping some students find the right publications to finish their projects. Andre was helping a school teacher figure out suitable textbooks she could recommend to her class while the head librarian, Mr. Novak, was relaxing in his office, listing to soft jazz and smoking his pipe. He justified this by convincing himself that the indoor smoking ban didn't apply to pipes and that an occasional pipe while hiding in his office was just fine. After all, he was the boss.

Luckily for Ana, she was shielded from the cold of the air conditioner by her beige and red coat. The plushness of her worn office chair increased the conduciveness of getting lost in a book.

Each page tugged Ana more and more into the story. She heaved aloud against her own library rules and settled her shoulders on the backrest yet again when the main characters of the book managed another narrow escape.

The effect of the book was hypnotizing enough for Ana not to see Andre sauntering up to her with a wide smile on his face. He dropped his big palm on her book, immediately fading the mesmerizing effect from her eyes. "Guess what?" Andre beamed.

"If it is not that you are going to remove your hand from my book, then I might have to bite it off."

"Oh, Ana. I hope this is not how you're going to be on your date tonight."

Ana stopped trying to read between his fingers and glanced up at him with widened eyes. "What do you mean, 'tonight'?"

Andre's air of confidence made Ana a little bit uneasy. His boldness was that of a person who had inside information. Or at least he knew something not yet made public. "Don't tell me it's what I'm thinking."

"Theo agreed to a date with you tonight."

"Theo?"

"The tutor guy."

"Tonight!? He hasn't even seen me yet." Ana was not trying to whisper anymore.

Andre sighed loudly, withdrawing his bulky hands from the book to retrieve his phone.

"In the real world, Ana," he chose his words slowly and gesticulated exaggeratedly, "people don't have to see you in person to like you. There is this thing called the internet, and he already knows your Instagram account."

"But the only things I post are my recent reads and quotes by my favorite artists."

"Well, aren't you lucky you found a nerd just like you?" He made a face at her. "But I do think you posted one picture of yourself."

"That was years ago when I was graduating from university."

"I think he liked it."

For some reason, Ana was torn between being cross at Andre for pairing her up that quickly with a stranger and being relieved that somewhere on the planet, there was an actual guy with the XY chromosomes that might be a match with her.

"Where are we going?"

"Your choice. He says he is willing to pick you up."

"No need, I will meet him in Gaststätte Birne."

"Roger."

●●●●●●●●

The night air was cooler, and Ana was grateful that she did not switch her windbreaker for something more stylish, as Andre suggested. She was opposite Gaststätte Birne with a piece of paper containing her date's phone number. One brief squint through the restaurant's window, and Ana could see who she thought could be Theo sitting at a corner table, wearing a blazer and white T-shirt. Not that Ana cared about fashion, but the clothes a person wore said a lot about them.

She quickly entered the number before her hands started to shake. She cross-checked the figures a fifth time before pressing the dial button. Sure enough, Mr. Blazer and T-shirt reached for the phone on the table and said hello. Ana greeted him courteously and proceeded into what she considered the most dreaded but anticipated part of her day.

●●●●●●●●

Ana had chosen the right place to meet. It was an old restaurant where she had never eaten before, but Theo seemed to be very acquainted with the establishment. He was familiar with every person that worked there.

"You seem to be popular here." Ana knew this was not the most entertaining of remarks, but it was better than the awkward silence she was facing.

"One of my favorite spots. Great choice for our first date," Theo said calmly with a grin.

Ana galloped to change the topic, anxious Theo would attempt to further define the nature of their meeting.

"Well, then, you could recommend me something from the menu?"

"Lamb is fantastic here! I heard they prepare it the way Hemingway used to like it. Maybe you want to try it, you know... him being one of your favorite writers."

Ana flinched. He really did check her Instagram profile. She definitely wasn't used to being seen.

"I would recommend a dry red wine with that; they have..." Theo continued but was interrupted without delay.

"I think I will go for a salad. And some freshly squeezed orange juice," she said, staring at the menu.

Theo shrugged, but the confident smile on his face promised he was just getting started on Ana.

At the end of the evening, Ana insisted on paying her part of the bill and excused herself with a platonic handshake. As she headed home in anticipation of her parents' reaction, Ana found herself blushing at the wet pavement as she strolled to the nearest bus stop. Theo was not just mildly good-looking, and they also had some kind of chemistry that she unsuccessfully tried to ignore. Theo looked at her like her hair was not just the same bird's nest it always was, and she noticed how the prettier girls in the restaurant did not sway his attention from their talk. But Ana did make a mental note to confront Andre about setting her up with a student when she wouldn't even date a man straight out of the university.

It was now time to walk away from the date to face her parents that night. Funnily enough, she was more reluctant to go back home than leave the restaurant where Theo was, even though she found out that he was still a student, meaning he was at least five years younger than her. From then on, it became a friendly chat between two like-minded individuals since Ana clearly expressed her thoughts about dating a younger man. A boy. Their conversation could have passed for a work chitchat or one of those group discussions school children have.

The next bus wouldn't come for half an hour. Ana checked her watch; it was 11:38 pm. She decided to walk. Going back to meet Theo for a ride back home was not really an option since, perturbed by taking a liking to Theo, she was avoiding him for now. He was still a student, for God's sake!

Most houses were already dark inside. But thankfully, the streets were moderately lit and safe. An old woman taking in her washing eyed Ana curiously. When Ana greeted her, the woman smiled and went indoors. *Friendly neighborhood*, she thought, chafing at the quietness.

The road led her onto a more deserted street. The loftiness of the apartment buildings tapered into bungalows as she advanced down the narrow road. The frequency of lit-up houses also faded as she proceeded.

She threaded further, hoping not to meet an unforeseen dead end. It was just then that she raised her head from the dim light of her phone to notice that many of the street lights were burned out or flickering towards their demise.

She hesitated to put on her phone flashlight, remembering to curse Andre under her breath because had she not wasted her time on a schoolboy, she would have been home and safely in bed reading by now.

Her flashlight swept across the streets and revealed a figure lying beside a waste bin by the corner of a vacant house that was being remodeled. It was the unmistakable silhouette of a human body, yet diminutive. The waste bin appeared to have been knocked over, spilling the content that now caught Ana's eye. *Is that a child? A mannequin?* She pointed the light directly on the body to reveal it was not made of flesh or plastic but of stone. "A marble statue," Ana gasped.

The librarian always wanted one, and there it was, staring back at her. The figure was the naked body of a woman from head to waist level, just below her belly button. The bosoms of the woman were rather full as they pointed forward like two eyes on her chest. Her belly was flat. A central line ran from between her breast to divide her midsection, showing that she was a very fit woman.

After examining those parts of her body, Ana was drawn to look at the face of the statue. She was young, beautiful, had full cheeks, and smiled cutely. She appeared to be in mid-blush while avoiding the gaze of her lover. Perhaps she was a model, and the sculptor himself was her love interest. The statue lacked arms which hurt Ana a lot because she would have loved to see how toned the hands of the fit woman would have been. She wanted to see her whole body.

The beauty of the well-polished marble shone as Ana's flashlight reflected off its surface. Ana moved closer to feel the cold stone. She touched it on the shoulder and then retrieved her hand. Then her inquisitiveness got the most of her, and she began to push through the garbage to find more interesting artifacts. She was like a kid in a candy store. Just that this particular store was already abandoned as waste. For some reason, somebody was throwing away good art, and she wanted to save the masterpiece. Unfortunately, it was too heavy to lift and haul all the way home.

Ana kicked through a pile of books that scattered around her feet and apologized to the papers like the ethical librarian that she was. On second look, the papers appeared not to be publications but a hand-written diary. From the look of the browned papers, she expected it to be from a long time ago. That would explain the ancient art.

Her curiosity led her to pull out any loose page of the book and gather it into the binder. Without thinking, she unzipped her laptop bag and added the recovered journal to the number of books she had taken from work.

As she stood up to continue her journey, a piece of paper fell from her hand and landed back onto the pile. She grabbed it again and read the lettering carefully. It was written in German. It was a purchase slip from 1981. Her eyes widened when they landed on the word "Sexspielzeug;" German for *sex toy*.

She hurriedly packed all the pages of the diary she could find into the black bin bag they spilled from. There was no more time to observe her findings on the dark street. If she wanted to get a better knowledge of the former owners, then she needed to take as much as she could home with her. Upon lifting up the heavy black bin bag, she found a woman's shoe, a man's shirt, and some other garments. Ana left those, presuming a mere knowledge of them being there would do her better than taking them home with her.

Flora was waiting up. "Your parents are asleep," she said when Ana stopped at her bedroom door. "They were sad that you could do anything to avoid spending more time with them."

Ana bit her lip and sat on the edge of Flora's stiff bed. "Well, they could have easily called or texted me if they wanted to spend time with me." Flora's eyebrows raised a question. "Anyway, they are the ones that said I should put myself on the market."

"Did you stand in the night waiting for a rich gentleman to pick you up in his Ford Mustang?" Flora's said with a throaty laugh.

Ana straightened her shoulders more seriously now. She looked her grandma in the eyes. "I went on a date this evening."

Seriousness returned to Flora's green-grey eyes. "A real date? With who?"

Ana shrugged, remembering Theo. "No one I will continue to see. I think I need a break from social events. I have to go to bed." She helped herself to her feet. "I need to be well rested for tomorrow."

Flora nodded as Ana bent to kiss her forehead, pretending not to see the black polythene bag Ana hid away at the door before entering her room. "Had dinner already, then?"

"Yes," Ana said, making her way out.

"Goodnight, dear. No pressure."

Ana turned and smiled. She sneakily picked the black nylon bag up and hid the recovered goods behind her bedroom door to be explored better in the daytime. After her routine bath and a few lines of a new novel, Ana was fast asleep.

●●●●●●●●

When Ana got to work the next day, she pulled out the tattered diary from her bag and remembered the whole incident of the night before.

Gabriella Meyer, 1987. Ana read the German scribblings on the page.

Everybody is scared. Will there be a war soon? Oh, I do wish I can tell what the outcome of this will be. I am writing this because I am scared too. I want to talk to somebody about what is going on with me and my husband, but I cannot talk to anyone because everyone else is scared too, and I don't know who I can trust.

If a war does break out, I will be grateful that I did not sit around just waiting for it to happen. I will do as much as I want to and document my life here for the time being. I hope this will satisfy me until the true outcome is fully determined.

Everybody is going ahead to do whatever in the world they can imagine to distract themselves from the truth. I am not like that. I will not take on meaningless activities just because I can, and I want everyone else to be like that too. If the wall is ever to fall, it should not result in swinish behaviors. It irritates me. Although I am not a communist, it does scare me to write this down, but I promise never to let anyone, even my husband, read this book.

My emotions are scattered here and there. I lost my flow of thoughts. It is a world where people who have been protected from a certain lifestyle are suddenly introduced to it. Everyone is having sex anywhere and with anyone.

Oh, how I wish that they were slowly introduced to the glory of sexual intimacy and love rather than all of a sudden being exposed to it.

They will not agree that West Berlin has had a negative effect on their sexual psychology, but I see it. I recognize it. In the West, it is unrestricted sex. Here, selling porno, and any form of public and media sex has been heavily frowned upon, prosecuted even. Could it be that in my time, the beauty of sexual intercourse will be so abused?

And no, I am not a communist. I am not a conventional East German. I honor no religion except the one that tells me to love my body and give it its pleasures. I am wholly against being trapped by the lusts of our desires.

I continue to advise and train and offer therapy to those struggling with connecting their mind to their bodies. I will do this till I die because it is my passion. I love to create a world where sex is free, meaningful, enjoyable, and spiritual. Not the taxi and club quickies that plague the land.

My husband and I are into this. The kind of love and affection we experience in our family bed. The intensity and understanding we share in it. I want to open the whole of Germany to such a level of knowledge of each other. And let them know that having such drive is not shameful, but neither is giving in to every urge desirable.

I see a world where me and my husband will live freely. We have always wanted to do this and now is our chance. We will continue to educate; for now, it will be as confidential as it can be, but once talks about a pending war clear, we will sensitize the masses of how blessed we are in our bodies to feel the sensation of love and touch in certain areas. I have my notes ready. I know the questions I must answer.

My goal is not about money. It could be everything but that. I still have a large inheritance from my father even though my husband, Bernd, had to quit his job because his coworkers did not like him.

Poor guy. They have not yet come to understand that being who he is did not make him less of a man. His clothes did not define his gender.

Yes, I share my clothes with him sometimes because he just loves to dress up in them. He prefers my shoes to his and likes to hold a purse rather than a briefcase. The senile idiots he worked with sent us death threats. I received a lot of them in the mail for one week straight until I finally let him quit. The harassment got to me.

2: DEEP SECRETS

"I received your text yesterday."

Ana shuddered at the male voice that came from above her, startling her. *Who in the world?*

"I really should have told you that he was in my brother's class too. A student tutor," Andre had his hands on his heart like it was a rehearsed apology.

"A student tutor?"

"I didn't think it was an important detail."

"You didn't think of telling me that the guy you set me up with was a student, five years younger, and entirely out of my stipulations for a life partner."

"Come on, Ana. You know he's not completely out of your stipulations. Both of you are the nerdiest people I have ever met. He was willing to overlook your style, so I just thought you could ignore his age."

"It was embarrassing, Andre. It really was. I had to politely excuse myself without hurting him. It could have gone one out of two ways. You should know how humiliating I felt being set up with someone I do not—"

"Yes, of course, I get it."

"It was a total evasion of my choices. I am not *that* desperate."

"You aren't? Ana honey, you are twenty-eight."

"And you're older."

"It's not the same."

"But it is. Your parents won't let you marry who you love, and my parents will never listen to me when I say I am not into the love thing or marriage."

Andre pulled a chair closer to Ana and took a seat right beside her. She was watching, wondering what she said that made him want to get comfortable to continue the conversation. It was still opening hours before the first bibliophile strolled in with book in hand. Ana decided to use those minutes to get familiar with Gabriella Meyer's story, but now, she was about to receive a sermon from her gay coworker.

"Stop avoiding it, Ana. You do not hate love or marriage."

"Never said I did, just—"

"I'm not done," Andre interrupted. "I know you don't hate love because when I told you about Theo, I saw the way your face lit up. I see the way you smile when that doctor comes in here and greets you."

"That's nothing. He is the most courteous library user in the whole of Lichtenberg. He does not leave his chair out, and he returns his book to the shelf and walks without dragging his feet. He obeys all of the library rules and respects people, even me."

"These are all part of the reasons why somebody can fall in love."

"No, I see it as mutual respect."

"It can also be that," Andre heaved and sat up straighter, "But it can also mean that you can fall in love, but you are not just allowing yourself to because you think you are not good-looking enough and nobody will ever love you for who you are?"

Ana bit her lips, rubbing her sweating palms on the lap of her black, ripped jeans. Her eyes darted to the clock, checking to see if it was time to open the doors. Earlier, she was looking forward to some private time before anyone else came in, but now, she was dying for a distraction to get Andre and her on their feet for any reason. Anything but sitting there, having an uncomfortable conversation.

"I can see you're getting uneasy."

She stopped creating friction between her palms and jeans.

"If this isn't what you want to talk about with your friend and colleague, then that's fine. But do not compare your lack of effort to my complicated dilemma. It just isn't fair." Andre stood up to leave. Ana muttered what she thought was an apology, but he didn't hear her. "And we need to get these books in order before Mr. Novak or anyone else gets here." He disappeared between the shelves.

How did an apology from him turn into me needing to apologize to him? she thought. Ana closed her book and took it with her to find him. He was in the geography books section, holding a mathematics textbook.

"That says geometry, not geography."

Andre checked the cover again. "Thanks," he said, going to find where the book really belonged.

Ana followed him. "I was being inconsiderate... what I said back there."

"Not a problem," Andre said in a not-so-high voice. "I really thought you would like Theo."

Ana smiled softly. "He was really interesting to talk to."

"Then text him. Honestly, I don't care if you two are not going to become a thing. You can just be friends. You could use one." Andre's tone was playful and cheery again.

Ana's smile broke into a wide grin. "Okay, I will." As she fumbled with her phone, the diary tucked under her other arm caught Andre's attention.

"Is that from here?"

Ana's eyes followed the direction his index finger was pointing to. "Uh no, it's not."

"I figured because I have never seen it around. What is it?"

"Nothing," she chimed, and he raised his eyebrows.

Ana found a place in her drawers to stash it until lunchtime, when she was free to read what she thought was the invasion of another woman's privacy. If she was going to be nosing into Gabriella's life, at least she could do her some courtesy and not share her personal business with everyone. Ana felt like this was her private quest and did not want it to become anybody else's matter.

•••••••

The notes were like lost letters written by a friend living far away in another time. Like secret letters from a mysterious acquaintance, Ana saw the diary entries as just that. It surely cleared her conscience when she poured over the pages like it was hers to see in the first place.

At lunchtime, Ana finally got her time away from the library. She stopped at Mr. Novak's office on her way out to inform him that she was going across the street to grab a sandwich, fully intending to use every second of her forty-five-minute break.

She waited at a window seat of the restaurant for her chicken sandwich. The lunchtime crowd poured into the small sandwich shop, but Ana took no notice of them. She found her place in the diary to discover that some pages were missing or misarranged.

Ana flipped until she found a comfortable place to continue. The words were scribbled in fine handwriting and there were no mistakes on the page like Gabriella had written her thoughts down on another paper and only copied them down in her diary.

Oleg was here again. He delivered just as much as we asked him to. But he demanded far more than we bargained. We had the money, so we gave it to him, but his fraudulence has to be checked. Maybe not by us because we are the people doing what nobody else will dare to do in East Berlin. It is scary but a huge leap of faith for me and Bernd. We know what we want.

You know how these Soviets are. Once you are helpless or you need their assistance in any way, they will dupe you of your money. Anything for their profit, especially when they know how desperate you are. Well, I do it not for myself. Bernd and I, we do it not for ourselves but for the community. That more will come to realize the sweetness of shared, consented, fleshly pleasure. That they will view it not as sin—as they have been convinced that coitus is—but adore it for the sheer privilege that it is.

The beauty of becoming somebody's desire is being pleasured and equally arousing pleasure on skin. The wonder that is the exploration of a body with your eyes, hands, and tongue. The sensuality of touching your skin on skin. Feeling the texture and the warmth. All these things make sex into what it is.

It is no surprise that East Germans have no idea how to cherish these acts. It has been abhorred by the media and schools. It is no wonder that West Germans tend to abuse the opportunity; too much of anything is not good. There is a moderate and worthy way to engage in sexual practices with your partner or with someone else upon their concurrence. The term we like to use is worship.

Worship is when your mind and utmost desire is not to seek your own gain but that of another. It is not about you. And when the two parties are not thinking about their organs, then sex becomes that of pure love rather than greed and lust.

Oh, and we are firm believers that one is well capable of loving more than one person at a time. Not just having two or more lovers at the same time but giving two of them the measure of affection that they each desire in the bed. Not deceptively, but with both of them being fully conscious that love does not diminish when there are more people to give it to. Energy may, but love never finishes.

In my sex therapy sessions, I try to convince women that their husbands loving another woman does not mean that they have stopped loving them. I want them to understand this. That the only things we have limited of are time and energy, never love. The problem should be that they might not have time to please them as before and divide attention fairly, and they will probably get worn out after being with the second woman. But if a man has gotten full control of how to love each woman the way they like, they should live together in harmony.

I refrain from using the word "equally" when talking about two women sharing a man. It is ignorance to assume that one woman will want him the way the other one will. That is hardly the case. I know women who want special attention just at night, and I know those who want it during every waking hour, except the time when they get ready for bed. If a man can get in control of his two women's needs, so far as they do not intersect in time or interfere with his energy levels for each woman, he will lead a peaceful polyamorous relationship or even marriage with two of them.

The same goes for a polyandrous woman. Just that there are much fewer of those. And fewer men are prone to share like women, who are naturally wired to permit.

To cure this issue with this woman and her husband, whom I will refrain from naming for her privacy, I ordered more sex toys from Oleg. I ordered more than necessary because many more women may be struggling with sharing their man with no way to ever voice their sorrows. Adult toys are the solution. I know it because the man need not exert too much energy when he is using it to love his woman. And furthermore, she may result to pleasuring herself when he is not available. This is not the main advantage but something that might suffice. A man can and will have more energy to please more than two women if she lets him use a toy.

The number of women unsatisfied in their sexual relationships scares me. What are men doing? Sometimes they just don't get it. It's amusing because women can get aroused by anything, even by sex between two males. I will admit to that.

Bernd knows this. This is why when we engage in swinging, he makes out with men. It turns me on. We prefer to swing than introduce a constant threesome partner. We do not condemn people who prefer threesomes, but we know many times it has broken relationships. Before we let any couple engage in one, we make sure they understand what they are about to do.

If my husband and I did believe in a god, we would be prayerful. This is a risk for me. I cannot fathom why I cannot close down my sex store. I don't know why I feel called to liberate women and men from meaningless one-night stands and to come into full knowledge of their selves. Men and women who fail to go through this will be doomed to sexless and unfulfilling romance. I also feel a duty to make couples in tune with each other's sexual needs.

Ana closed the book and stared at the wrinkled, leather front cover. *Am I in tune with my body?* she thought. Her thoughts were interrupted by an employee waving to her like he was motioning to a deaf person. It surely wasn't her who he was waving at. He easily could have been waving to someone outside. She looked back through the glass window and saw no one on the other side. Then she realized, *My sandwich!*

She spent the rest of her lunchtime eating her sandwich and reading the diary. She searched through the loose pages, not knowing what she was looking for but with a gut feeling that when she located it, she would know.

Her triumph did not take too long to arrive. She was staring at a page with a numbered list on it. Ana took a bite of her sandwich and read the first words on the page. "Steps to getting to know yourself sexually." She checked her near environment, and when she was convinced that nobody was looking at her or could see the handwriting in the book she held, she continued reading.

The first thing on the page was to find a private place to do the exercise. A window seat in a fast-food restaurant on the side of a busy street did not cut it as a private environment, but Ana kept reading. After the knowledge was acquired, she would do whatever Gabriella recommended in her bedroom that evening. With every line she read, Ana grew more and more confident in the woman whose life's work she now had access to.

Gabriella told her to close her eyes and imagine a lover. Not any lover she had been with, but an imaginary character if possible. Gabriella suggested a crush she never got a chance with. Or a celebrity she thought was sexually attractive. Ana found her mind drifting towards Theo. She shook her head and tried to remember a celebrity crush, but the last time she had one of those was when he was sixteen, and unfortunately, thinking of a younger Justin Bieber did not particularly feel good.

OK, Theo, you are only going to do this with me in my imagination and not in real life. She wondered if Theo was also using her the way her thoughts used him. She tried to envision it, but it irked her.

The next thing Gabriella suggested was to imagine being in your happy place. Ana was in the library. Theo was standing at the door in all the glory of a college boy's body.

Tanned, chiseled, sexy in dim lights that highlighted his undulating ripped abdomen. "Gosh!" But it was not Ana who said this. And it was not Theo either.

Recognizing the voice, she flung her eyelids open and gazed around for the owner of the words. Andre was plopped down on a chair he dragged to her table. He had a grin spinning all around his head as he grabbed the diary from Ana's hands.

Theo and the dimly lit library evaporated from her mind's eye.

"What are you doing with this book?" asked Andre. "It's not from out library."

"I think the real question is, 'what are you doing here?'"

"You mean, what am I doing in my usual lunch eatery during my break?" She snatched the fragile book back from Andre's.

"Check the time, Ana. Your break ended twenty-five minutes ago."

He could not have been correct. It was just thirty minutes in when she started finding herself. Then Ana discovered how long it took her to find a perfect partner to do the exercise with in her head. "That doesn't mean you should take what's not yours and read. It's very invasive."

"Hey." He let his hands do the talking along with his lips. "I did not know it was a highly classified text."

"Yeah, right," Ana said. She tucked the book under her arm and munched a big bite from her forgotten lunch.

"Come on, Ana. You know this is not the first time you've gotten lost in a book, and I've had to fetch you from here. I always check what new fascinating read you have been lost in, and today just happened to be one of those days. And Mr. Novak said that we will have to start taking our breaks together."

"What?"

"Yes. From now on, he is giving us the same break time. The library will be locked up until we return," he paused, "together."

"I won't get any alone time?"

"That is precisely the goal."

"What?"

"Eat up, miss." He laughed, stirring to stand up soon.

Ana stuffed her mouth and wondered how much of Gabriella's diary entries Andre saw. "What did you see?"

Andre picked himself up and squinted at her face.

"Be honest, Andre," she said, begging more than demanding.

"I saw nothing! But I am dying to find out what it is, girl!" It became clear that curiosity got the best of Andre.

Ana stared at the table.

"Come on, let me see," Andre was putting his hands out for Ana to hand over the diary. She playfully slapped his hands with it while latching on to it. Surprisingly, Andre was playing it cool but only for a moment. He bounced up from his seat, and during what seemed to be a tickling attack on Ana's belly, he ripped the diary away from Ana's hands and opened the page where Ana inserted a napkin. Ana knew better than to try to take the diary back. Rather, buried under layers of embarrassment, she watched Andre, eyes and mouth wide open, devour Gabriella's instructions on self-pleasuring. He wasn't mocking Ana like she expected him to. His laughing at her would be the last thing she wanted, but it never came. He handed the diary back as if he understood he had crossed the line.

Sitting in the hard wooden chair for so long caused Ana's legs to fall asleep. Still not diverting her gaze from the wooden tabletop, she struggled to stand. Andre offered a helping hand, but Ana waved him away. She put her body weight on her paralyzed legs. Her feet failed to support her, and she buckled at her knees, falling onto the chair and then rolling onto the floor.

"Ana!"

Great. More reasons to be embarrassed, she thought to herself, scowling.

●●●●●●●●

If Mr. Novak was angry, he didn't show it. They found their way into the main library hall, easing him back to his office. Ana often wondered if there were so few library employees because that is what the government could afford to pay or because there were rarely more than a handful of library visitors. Other public libraries had an array of staff on duty all day.

She glanced at Andre as he was scanning borrowed and returned books for the library database. His hands moved fast, and his eyes were fixed on the screen. It was her who was constantly fidgeting, thinking that he was watching her. *Oh, why won't he talk about what he read in the diary?*

She tried to keep her eyes on the laptop screen in front of her. The library was empty. It usually took some time to be filled in the afternoon hours. The influx of visitors peaked in the morning, immediately after the doors opened, and at the 4:30 pm rush hour when school children and corporate workers were dismissed.

"Uhh, Ana. I see that a certain book was borrowed and returned, but I did not find the book on the shelf when I checked."

"If it is the Colleen Hoover novel, I took it."

Andre faced her. "You naughty little thief."

"Naughty?" she almost screamed. Ana scanned Andre's face for a hint of mischief. His squinting squeezed the skin on his forehead. A sigh escaped her parted lips. Waiting for Andre to taunt her was more invigorating than running a sprint. "So, you're not going to say anything about the book?"

"Huh? Oh, the self-stimulating thing. I did it way back when I found out I was gay. It was in sex therapy, though, and he recommended that I do it in a private place. I don't know what your therapist advised." He chuckled.

"She is not *my* therapist. And I'm sure you read where she advised the same thing."

Andre's chuckling got louder. "So, you decided to do yours in front of a bunch of people."

"I was not yet doing it. Just preparing for when I could."

He opened his mouth like he was about to say something, but he didn't.

"You wanted to ask me who I was thinking about, right?"

"No, I just wanted to ask you where you found a collection of handwritten sex therapy notes if she is not your therapist. That shit is illegal to publish."

"Not if the names are hidden and only the nitty-gritty of the session is written down. Plus, she didn't publish it. This is her diary."

Andre jerked. "You are reading the diary of a sex therapist?"

Ana's eyes opened wider. "No, no, no, it is not like that. See, Gabriella is a friend, and she writes me letters sometimes. You know how terrible I am with romantic stuff. She is nice and really wants to help."

"You are not just terrible with romance but also lying." Ana was about to protest. "I know all the friends you have."

"Well, this one is from college. She studied psychology and majored in sex education."

"Hmm." Andre folded his hands and nodded. "She's helping you?"

"Yes."

"But you don't have a therapist."

"Not exactly."

Andre pretended to go back to work, but Ana knew he was not finished drilling her for the truth. The way he bit his lips, making audible pondering sounds. After every "hmm" and "aha," Ana jolted, wondering if he remembered something else she said that could implicate her, but he was scanning the book codes faster and arranging them onto a cart that would help him take them to their destinations on the library shelves. Ana waited.

"I say you stole the book."

"Did not. That is so not my character."

"But it is," he smiled, pointing at his computer screen.

"This is different, okay?"

"Yes, it is. In this case, you are not the custodian of that sex therapist's logbooks. It was not published, and I presume you have no intentions of returning it." Andre typed as he spoke. Ana stared at him. "Or them," he said.

"Pardon?"

"Who is to say if you took only one of the books. I know you, your curiosity, or rather, greed for knowledge, could make you misappropriate more than one book at a time." He smacked his lips. "Oh, look here, another missing novel by Paulo Coelho, and it is not recorded that it was ever borrowed."

"What is your point, oh wise sage?" Ana lashed out.

"That you took what doesn't belong to you, and you ought to respect people's privacy like you are fond of chanting."

"This is a different case, Andre, okay? I tried to tell you. I didn't steal this book, and I can't return it."

"Why?"

"Because she's dead!"

They were both breathing very fast now but for different reasons. A vein that traveled from Ana's forehead to her neck throbbed like it could burst any second. Andre was panting. "Dead?"

"Excuse me," Ana said, getting up from her seat and heading to the shelves. Andre, her friend, accused her of being a thief. How could he think that of her? The day had been filled with a whirlwind of emotions right from the time when she checked into the library to vexing Andre, then being embarrassed in the restaurant, and now she was furious that Andre knew about Gabriella's book and accused her of stealing it.

There, between shelves filled with astrology books and modern literature, Ana began to cry. It was the only thing she knew how to do when there was a mix of emotions she could not bear. The tears rolled down her cheeks like hot water from the shower. She perched herself on one of the empty base shelves and brought her face to her folded knees, wrapping her arms around them.

"I'm sorry, Ana."

Andre hovered over her in silence. The whole library was silent but for the sporadic sniffing coming from the back shelf. He paced, and she remained seated there, not showing him her face or acknowledging his presence.

"I know how it feels, Ana. I know how it feels because I was once there." He slowed down his pacing until it was checkered with halts in the middle of his steps. "I was also confused about my sexuality. I know you are not like me; yours is different. You may be wondering many things, like why you are not interested in love and all."

The sniffing stopped as he droned on. Ana was looking at him now, but he was too busy giving his speech to realize that. "Andre." Her voice was not as smooth as she wanted it to be, but at least it called his attention. "Stop." He positioned himself better to see her clearly. "Just stop. Stop trying to figure me out. Stop trying to be so helpful. You've done enough."

His squeaky voice said something that Ana did not hear. She tore into him. "Don't you see what is happening here? First Theo and then this?"

"Ana, I just want to help."

"No! You have done enough!"

He could not imagine for the life of him what made Ana flare up like that. "I want to know more about your sex therapist, that's all."

Ana decided to let the cat out of the bag. She told him about the marble statue she left behind despondently, the paper slip revealing an acquisition of sex toys, and, finally, the disarray of what used to be Gabriella's diary. The captivating mystery. The inviting reading, she cannot resist.

There was silence, so Andre stole the opportunity to talk. "I know you will be doing your research to find her or whatever, and I want to join you."

Ana was dumbstruck. She ran her hand through her thick hair. Of everything she expected Andre to say, this was not it. Finally, she relaxed her tensed muscles and nodded at him as she took her leave. Whatever the nod meant to him, she did not know, she did not care.

He followed behind her to the place where their quarrel started. They worked in silence till the close of the day. Ana had enough time to think about the proposal Andre made. However, the funny setting and very informal posture might have aggravated her anger. On second thought, he had a car and was far more knowledgeable of the history and the streets of Berlin.

She picked up her oxblood laptop bag after ensuring the two novels she picked this time around were still in it. This night, she was determined to read them in her bedroom, no matter what her parents had to say to her.

It was evening, and she knew that walking would take much of her reading time, and so would waiting for the bus. She hated to ask, but she needed Andre to drive her home.

"Hey, Andre."

He turned around, puzzled. Ana was also shocked by her behavior, but she found herself asking for a ride home.

"Does this mean you forgive me?"

"Yes."

"Does this mean you will let me in on the mission?"

"You are more excited than you should be. You think it's bigger than it is."

"But don't you want to find out who wrote the book?"

"Gabriella did."

"And what do you know about her and what happened to her sex store. Don't you know about East Germany and their unrealistic hatred for venereal appearances?" Andre was smiling like a kid in a candy store on Christmas morning. There was no barrier to his ecstasy.

They were interested in different parts of the mystery. Ana was in love with Gabriella's boldness and vision for her work. Andre cared about all the other things that surrounded it. She brought her mind back to the present, seeing how Andre could make a good team partner. After all, they were coworkers in the library, and they did good work.

"If I say you can join me, will you finally take me home?"

"Sure!" His eyes beamed.

Ana stretched out her hand for a handshake. Andre took it and pulled her into a tight hug. In that moment, she forgot about the fight they just had. The terrible things she felt and how she questioned her sexuality, as Andre rightly analyzed. And for the moment, she was in the arms of her friend, who understood her the way no one else did.

3: HEDONISTIC PLEASURE

I love when my husband and I do the things we do best. Yesterday, it was in the living room. He got back from the garden outside with the most beautiful tulips and stored them in the perfect glass vase that he bought for me on my last birthday. It stayed in the kitchen cupboard for almost a year, but now it has found use. My husband was looking very handsome that dawn.

I often say that it is the littlest things couples do for each other that rekindles interest. For me, yesterday, it was his dirty hands and stained shirt. Bernd is quite the handyman. I love it when he does the minutest things, like changing the lightbulb and fixing up something in the shed. I love it when I can smell the sun on his clothes and when his skin glistens with moisture.

I was not in the mood before he showed up. He owned and looked after the only home garden the neighborhood had, and it was ours. My Bernd was not like other men. He did not shun beautiful activities like growing flowers or relegate domestic activities to me alone. He was quite the assistant.

After he left the pink glass vase containing pink tulips on the mantle, he turned around to meet the most beautiful thing he had ever seen in his life. I am still the most beautiful woman. I hate being vain, but I know that even though I am not in the same shape I was when he met me, my body is still curved at all the right places. I've never had a child, so the familiar stripes on the skin of mothers, the "bloatedness" and the fallen breasts, my body has never seen. I was wearing a thin chiffon robe. Black with red flowers and green leaves. His eyes glowered over me until he was able to focus on the buxom body of his wife after spending time out in the sun. I think I heard him say, "delicious." He disappeared into the corridors to the room for a while. I knew he was freshening up for our exotic evening, but I did not know how long it would last.

We started by around 5:40 because I remember the television program I was watching that evening aired by that time. I was surprised when we both receded from each other, panting like big cats after their wild chase and drifting off into the dream world. I checked the grandfather clock we have in our living room to discover that it was well past 10 pm.

We expended a lot of energy during our back and forth with thrusts and positions that neither of us was strong enough to fix anything for dinner. These are the times when I am most grateful that we don't have any children. If we did, who would have fixed dinner for them? Would we have had to cut our time short just so that they could eat? And if we had children, would we not be constrained to the bedroom for our playful activities instead of being able to do it anywhere in our big house.

Don't get me wrong, I love children, sometimes I wish I would have had my own, but other times, I am grateful not to be tied to the responsibility that comes with having them. I love my neighbor's—our landlord's kids. We are rich enough to get our own house, but you know this place, once you start building, everyone is alert, trying to poke around to figure out where you get your money from. We don't mind living below our means because even though we do not get all our money from our sex shop and my sex therapy, exposing ourselves to prying eyes will get us in trouble. So, we live in a rented apartment.

I am presently laughing as I am writing this because of how "off course" I have gone. I started with writing about last night, and I have found myself talking about children. That is a story for another day. Anyway, so as Bernd came back wearing only his tight, white briefs—I love those on him—he walked up behind me and gave me a peck on the cheek.

He cupped my face and leaned forward. I smelled his cologne—a strong, alluring scent. He pecked me again, and this time, I pecked him back, still looking at the television. He needed a stronger attempt to break my attention from the screen, so he started kissing my neck and sucking behind my ears. That is my weak point. I giggled a bit, feeling the tingling sensation.

He went further and bit my earlobe softly, his tongue dancing around the circumference. I bit my lips to keep my excitement from showing. His hands went further to massage my shoulders while he still kept biting and sucking and kissing my right ear, neck, and shoulder. Then he took it to the other shoulder. At this point, I could not keep my moans inside my throat. He massaged my shoulders and extended his hands lower and lower.

I threw my head back so that he could see what he was doing to me. Our eyes met, and in a split second, our lips were between each other. Our upside-down French kiss lasted with a lot of pausing to breathe. Our mouths devoured each other. I always love it when Bernd shows just how much he loves me with his tongue.

Bernd controlled the kiss. He owned it. Our heads turned this way and that, but his lips did not lose grip with mine. When he had enough, his strong hands slipped lower still. He cupped my breast. It was then that my second most enjoyable thing about sex started. The dirty talk.

He asked me if I liked it, and I nodded. His hands cupped my large breasts and let go of most of it but my nipples. My breasts are on the big side, so they jiggled *when he played with them. I tried to relax all my muscles to enjoy the moment but also ended up tensing everything because of how good it felt.*

I could not keep myself from moaning. His fingers were at work on my nipples, twisting them while his breath caressed my cheeks. I raised my arm and put them around his neck. He got the signal and came around the long chair to face me. In a single breath, he scooped me from my butt, and I saddled my legs around his waist.

Bernd is tall but not very muscular. He is also not lanky.

I clasped my arms around his neck and tried to keep myself from slipping off. I must confess that I do not really enjoy that position because I have to put in so much energy not to fall. I prefer when the man is doing most of the work during sex. I like to be pampered, and Bernd knows this. He tried to support me with his strong arms under my butt. We kissed—slight pecks on the lips until he let me down and started taking off my clothes.

As he pulled my top off, I fastened my fingers around the waist of his tighty whities and gave it a yank. It revealed his already hard penis. I left him looking down at me, shocked at my speed. My breasts were already bare and exposed—I don't like to wear bras all the time. I bit my lips and shrugged as he kept staring down at me, a smirk pulled at the left side of his cheek. He asked me if I just couldn't wait for him. I could not answer. I just stayed there, smiling up at his beautiful big eyes.

He picked me up again, but this time, he let me stand. He let my hair fall as he pulled it back with his hands, raising my head. Bernd liked that. I also let him pull it down. It gave some form of sweet hurt. A mixture of pleasure and pain. My eyes were perpetually looking up. All I could see were the features on his tanned face. Then he stopped pulling and started combing my hair with his fingers. He ran his hands through, tugging at the roots and letting my hair tangle with his digits at the tips.

I whispered his name and whispered some more that I loved it, and I loved him. He did not want to stop hearing that because, from the way he kept on combing and watching for my reaction, he yearned to keep pleasing me. His hands left my hair and traveled down my bare back to my bottom. He squeezed it, but that was not the final destination.

One of his palms gathered the hem of my skirt together and pulled it up. The other one slipped up, maneuvering my underwear until he could feel my aroused vagina. I can't remember how now, but after he caressed me down there, I was on the chair again, and he was slipping my skirt off.

I bit my lips hard when he finally took it off. We were staring into each other's eyes lovingly, wantonly. We collapsed into each other's arms, rubbing our bare bodies together. I don't know why I can't recall much of what happened after that. I know he fingered and licked me and brought me to an orgasm before inserting his penis into my hole.

At this time, I think it was just a few minutes before 7 pm. We spend a lot of time in foreplay because we understand how necessary it is in enjoying the length of sexual intercourse. My Bernd is the most compassionate fellow I have ever been with. I can say that because we engage in swingers' parties, and I notice how other men are too swift to do penetration without cunnilingus. They care more about putting their penises in other women's mouths without considering if she is even aroused enough for fellatio to excite her.

Those are the kind of things that put me off during sex. When a man rushes to receive pleasure rather than to give it. My man is more feminine when it comes to his sexual gestures. He cares, he asks questions, and he does not stick his penis into my mouth without prior warning. He also doesn't ask for it when he knows I have not gotten to that point yet. When I do, I'm often the one that takes it myself.

After thrusting in the sitting position—I was under him, sitting on my low back and the top of my butt with only my shoulder and head resting on the backrest while he hovered over me, resting his weight on his arms that were on the chair at both sides of my body. His legs also extended beyond the chair and supported him on the ground.

I felt myself getting closer to orgasm, so I quickly turned around to change position. He was on the chair now, where I pushed him to. I knelt down in front of him and glanced up at him. His breathing was epileptic, his eyes begged me for what he knew was coming, and I took his penis in my hand then, slowly brought it to my mouth, kissed, licked, then flicked my tongue on the tip.

Air escaped from his mouth noisily. His chest pumped up and fell as I continued to use my hands and mouth to pleasure him. He touched me at the back of my head, sending chills down my spine. I gasped, but as I did, he took me by my cheek and brought me up. His lips smashed with mine. Later, I was back on my knees, pumping my head up and down while feeling and watching him squirm from the corners of my eyes.

Ana swiveled in her chair. The library was closed on Sundays, and it was the only day of the week that she could sit at home all day and get into Gabriella's book without distractions. Her parents were on their way to Italy for yet another fashion week. Ana thought of Theo and flinched. She scrunched her eyebrows together when she tried to remember if his name was Theophilus or Theodore. Theodore was definitely the better name.

She focused her gaze back on the yellowing leaves of paper that Gabriella told her life story on. Her handwriting and spacing were consistent all through each page. It made Ana remember learning calligraphy writing in secondary school. Gabriella's cursive snaked around the sheet, small letters joining wherever they could.

Ana imagined Gabriella sitting at her desk in the middle of the night after enjoying Bernd all through the evening. She would be gathering her nightgown in her lap so that she could sit comfortably and document the experience. Ana pictured Gabriella as a small but buxom woman in her early forties. She was tender and cared a whole lot about household duties. Her husband was also the same as her in that aspect.

Bernd was pictured as a tall, buff mannequin of a man who cared more about his looks than other men Ana has known. Even Andre, and that is a hard feat to beat. Bernd was not ambitious like other men. He married into wealth because he could not go on working in toxic environments that put pressure on him to perform more than he was mentally wired to think was required.

He, too, must have grown up in a very protective family. Gabriella never made mention of his upbringing, but Ana suspected that he did not get the burden of "being a man" from home.

They met after school. That was as much as Ana knew about Gabriella and Bernd's earliest association. He was working, but she wasn't as she never had. They fell in love, and Ana could guess that their views on sexuality and love played a huge role in tying them together in their matrimonial bond.

Flora was out—in the market or at a friend's to visit. For breakfast, Ana had bread with chicken, lettuce, and cream cheese, but not in sandwich form. She had a plate of lettuce doused with cream cheese on one side, a saucer containing chicken, and a loaf of sliced bread on her work desk. Sometimes she spread cream cheese on a slice and added chicken and lettuce, other times, she bit the bread, took a few spoons of minced lettuce and cream cheese, and topped it up with a piece of chicken from the bone.

A message made her phone chime. It was from Theo. She read it, and it was something about him wanting to meet up with her after church. At the same time, Andre sent a text message complaining about how his mother forced him to go to church with her. Ana was glad that she could live with her parents and do anything she wanted. She paused to think about it. She was not really free to stay single and be in her parents' home, so it was almost the same.

She sent Andre a sad emoji accompanied by: "Living with our parents now feels like when we were kids."

She opened Theo's message knowing well that he would be aware that she read it.

"I'm going to need you to stay away from me," she said out loud in response to Theo's message.

We planned a steamy swingers' party. It was a little impromptu. What I'm saying is that I have friends who are ready for this, no matter what. They will never reject an opportunity for things like this. And, like I always say, sex is not a game. I don't condone teenagers and adults—especially men—treating it like it was just another board game, like chess.

Sex—when hallowed for what it is—brings two people closer together. Sometimes, sex heals broken relationships. And that is where this swingers' party got its relevance.

My friend, an optician, and his wife had a falling out months ago that badly affected their relationship. I believe it had to do with a sickness the woman had, but they denied it, saying it was more intense than that, emotional distress, they argued. I let it fly and suggested a swingers' party.

Here is what it was supposed to do, voyeurism. It is the sexual measure that one gets from watching another person engage in sexual activities. The optician, who I will not name for privacy's sake, seems to be aroused from watching women disrobe or making sexual moves when they are half naked.

For women, I know we can get turned on by watching anyone have sex. A partner, a friend, strangers, shadows, two women, two men, apes... so I suggested a large orgy. My number one goal was to strengthen the relationships that were present there. It was no flimsy exercise done just for the measure of it, but a premeditated, tactical approach to restore a bleeding marriage.

We met in my sitting room. We were not that many. Just eight of us. Me and Bernd, the optician, and his wife. A lesbian couple and a gay couple. I thought it was necessary to mix it up a bit like that. It is also more exciting to have a variety of sexualities.

Bernd had no issues getting into something with the gay men. I watched him more than I folded with other participants. But for the reason of not appearing too saintly, I'll be honest. I touched the girls. I did not let them lick me or get too physical, but I was physical with the men.

At some point, I could not keep my eyes open. I did not see Bernd nor the optician that was thrusting in and out of me, nor did I see the girls trying to fight him off so they could take over. I was out. My eyes went blank. I was staring into nothingness. At some point, I stopped hearing the moans of the two gay men. I believe they went upstairs. I didn't care. I could feel, but I could not see.

Bernd took over at a point. I know my man when he touches me. I felt his hand slide from my neck down to my boobs, then to my navel, and up again. Then he repeated it with his other hand. My breath changed, then he started ramming into me.

That was all the night was about. We got dressed when morning came, and the day was bright. I did not see the two gay men anymore, but I just believed that they left earlier.

What I am happy about the most was that it was able to bring my two friends closer together sexually. Somehow, seeing his wife enjoy being loved by other people sparked a need in him to see his wife the way she is—a beautiful gem that should be admired and loved.

A call came through; it was Theo. He was done with the church for the afternoon, and it was then Ana who realized that she had not done anything that day but pour over Gabriella's writings. There was a lot of clothing and loose sheets of paper littering the floor, but that was not what Ana was looking at.

The phone stopped ringing, and Ana returned to her silence and could think. The polythene bag was still in the corner of her room. The one containing large clusters of documents and the receipt of the sex toys Gabriella ordered from Oleg, the Soviet supplier.

Ana questioned Gabriella's morals at the moment. Sex was her solution to every relationship issue. And it was more than sex. Sometimes it was swingers' parties; sometimes it involved a third party and having a threesome. Ana loathed the idea but not fully because her next thought was to invite Theo over and get physical with him, maybe then she will be able to look past his age, and he would love her no matter how she looked. But Ana was not about to ruin her life to test Gabriella's trustworthiness.

Theo called again, and this time, she picked up. "I'm home," she said.

"No church for you today, I suppose."

"Nope."

"I was hoping we could meet up, maybe get ice cream or something cold, you know days are getting warmer—"

"I'm fine," she said with a tone of finality. Would a good Christian boy agree to have sex with her just so she could test Gabriella's theories? she thought as she turned him down.

"Oh. I'll get back to you later. It sounds like this isn't a good time."

The line cracked with air gushing out from Ana's mouth. She had her eyes closed because she realized what she had just said. "I didn't mean to—"

"It's fine," Theo reassured her.

"I like you, Theo."

The air froze. Ana shut her eyes tighter and banged her palm on her forehead. Her lips were held in place between her teeth.

"Do you mean that, Ana?"

"I mean, I think I do."

There was a pause.

"Wanna have ice cream with me then?"

"Where? Your campus?"

"Very funny, Ana. Tell me where you live so that I can pick you up."

She bit her lips and spilled her address. In less than forty minutes, she had taken her bath, brushed her teeth, styled her hair in a way she thought was presentable enough, and slipped on a sundress. She left the big hat because she thought it was too fancy and might make her look like she was trying too much. Then she contemplated taking the shades but wearing them on her bushy auburn locks might look too extravagant, and clipping them to the neckline of her dress would hinder her cleavage from showing the way she wanted it to. It was a floral dress that her mother had bought years ago. It was short for her when she first tried it, and it still was, but Ana was not the same person that afternoon.

Maybe if she looked pretty enough, she could have him home with her, and then he would love her and never leave her. Maybe they could be a thing. Her fears were not that he was younger anymore. It was the fear of being rejected, it was always that, but she looked for an excuse, something other than her insecurities to blame it on.

"Hey, Andre, I am getting ready for a date with Theo. It's weird. But before I thank you, I have to know how this turns out." She pressed send. Then she immediately started to type out another text to Andre, "Okay, it's not like a date per se. We are just going to get ice cream. That's a date—"

His reply came in before she was done typing that. "Wow, this is surprising. How did he talk you into giving him a second chance? You go, girl!"

She laughed, envisioning him throwing his arms in the air and praising her like it was such a big deal that she scored herself a second date.

Then she went a step further and confessed, "I want to get laid."

She waited for Andre's response and got none. Overthinking made her regret sending that. She left the phone on her desk and distracted herself by staring into the mirror. Her lips looked dry. A quick lip gloss application fixed it. Andre called.

As soon as he heard the call connect, he said, "You want what?"

"To get laid."

"Why? I mean, how?"

"No reason. It's just something that crossed my mind. How do I do that?"

Andre caught himself from speaking too quickly. He laughed nervously. "You are ready to have sex with him?" Ana smacked her lips.

"Come on now, Ana. Tell me what this is all about."

Ana told him about the cases Gabriella tried to solve in the diary she was reading. Cases of couples not talking with each other that sex solved, an individual not feeling loved, a distasteful and ending marriage. Sex seemed to be the solution to all that. At the end of her narration, Andre was exasperated. "What can I say?" he said.

Ana heard a horn honk twice cheerfully, and she was sure it was Theo.

"Oh my gosh, Theo's here. Let's take this online. I really need you to tell me what to do."

"Okay, Ana," Andre said with a reprimanding undertone. "But what do you want to solve here?"

"I want to be loved."

Ana hastily stuffed her shades, some sunscreen, and lip gloss into her bag, and then she made her way out the front door to meet a smiling Theo, still in his church attire. He complimented her house, and Ana acted like she did not know it was big and beautiful.

4: A TERSE MOMENT

From somewhere in the library came a muffled cough, a raspy and jagged screech that made Ana imagine metal being scraped against metal. There was a general rule of silence in the library; it was posted on all the shelves, walls, and desks.

But coughing couldn't be counted as breaking the law or transgressing the rule. But she looked up still, her neck craned like a mother straining to hear sounds from her child's court. Ana didn't know why she looked up in that moment, but if she put thought to it, she knew that it would be either because she was bothered by the shattered stillness or simply because she was human. By the time she found the source of the cough, she had discovered that she wasn't the only one looking. She was just one of the pairs of eyes that were attracted to the sound that had slowly become a distraction in the large hall.

When her eyes landed on the cougher, for a moment, she was petrified by shock. The hair, the shape of the head, and the hunch of the shoulder reminded her of Theo, transporting her back to the ice cream date.

Was he here? Did he intend to attract her attention with his cough? No. No. No. Not now, Ana thought to herself.

She asked herself as she gazed at him, her finger placed in between the pages of the diary on her desk. A wedge to track her progress, a landmark to mark where she last stopped. She couldn't afford to miss out on the journey, the tales of Gabriella and Bernd. She was already subsumed in that world, a fly caught in the web.

Her questions were soon answered when the figure stood up from his seat and hurried out of the room, a white handkerchief pressed to his face, his free hand stuck in his pocket, back hunched like someone aware of the ruckus they had started. The sounds of his footsteps made weird knocking noises on the floor. Noises that seemed too loud in the too-quiet room. It wasn't Theo.

Good gracious, she mused.

The rapid flutter of wings that had started in her chest slowed. Even her rapid breathing decelerated. She would have gone back to her book, returned to the past, to the house of sex, Gabriella and Bernd's little abode, if not for the slight buzz that had begun in the room, the beginnings of gossip.

Immediately, a frown appeared on her face, and she got up like a teacher with the intention of restoring the sanity of raucous students. Even as she walked, she knew that she wouldn't need to speak, wouldn't need to mention anything to the chattering and sniveling folks. All she would need is to walk toward them, and sanity would be restored. And that is exactly what happened. The room fell silent at the sight of her, even if she knew that as soon as her back was turned, tongues would hang out, and eyes would roll in false mockery. She knew this because she had seen it done to Andre before, and she had also done it when she was younger to many librarians. Didn't they say what goes around comes around? She smiled as this thought crept into her head. She didn't mind. What she did mind, what dominated her thoughts, was the diary that lay open and facedown on a desk like an upturned bowl.

She couldn't remember when last a book, or anything at all, had held her in a vise grip ever the way this diary has. The last time she had felt something like she was feeling now was when she was reading *Game of Thrones*. She had told herself that she would pair it with the two other books that she was reading at that moment. Reading multiple books at the same time was one of her quirks. It had been like that ever since she was a child, or ever since she could remember falling in love with books. But as soon as she flipped open the first page of that book, she couldn't find a way, a chance to fulfill that promise of hers. And it was the same way that she felt about the diary.

Ana sank into her chair as noiselessly as she could as soon as she returned to her desk. Immediately, her hand found the diary. It felt as though her hands were magnets, and the diary was a chunk of metal. Like a ravenous wolf, like Jon Snow's dierwolf Ghost in *Game of Thrones*, she dug into the diary immediately.

In my life, there have been many events that have occurred. Many of them have disappeared into the places where memories go, but there are others, others like the summit of the mountain that stands out from a distance or like branded skin markings and tattoos. This day was one such. But I didn't know then. I wouldn't have known. How would I? I am no witch, no soothsayer. There was no way I would know. The morning had started like a typical morning. The sun had risen as it should, slowly but brightly, like a child playing hide and seek behind the clouds. The sounds of early morning had slowly filtered into our house—the sounds of crying babies, entreating mothers, and moving vehicles. This was all I heard when I woke up. I am no early riser, but I'm also not a late riser, so I must have woken up about the time that I always do. Which is always between seven and nine o'clock. Like every normal day with no inkling of what would happen, of what was coming, I went about my daily ritual—face washing, teeth brushing, preparation of a light breakfast. We are not heavy eaters.

In movies, it is common to see victims, or the protagonist who meets their doom, notice things, clues, that if they had paid attention to, would have saved them. But I didn't see any. Perhaps I didn't pay attention; perhaps there wasn't any to be seen.

So, the morning progressed as it should. We had a breakfast of scrambled eggs, bacon, and coffee. Like couples in love, the breakfast was an affair of gazing at each other, talking about the events of the past, and the plans for the day with mouths filled with food. "You should finish up before you talk," I remember saying to Bernd with my mouth brimming with partly chewed bacon. Talk about not practicing what I preached. I remember us laughing at this, our eyes brimming with mirth and affection. Our hands reaching out to touch each other's to form a link that showed externally what we felt for each other internally—an unbreakable love. Our times together were always like this, it wasn't just about the intimacy of the breakfast; it was the intimacy of all times, all our times together.

Later, when I kissed Bernd goodbye, I saw in his eyes a sparkle and a longing. "I can't wait to see you when I get back," was what the look said. "I can't wait to see you also," I replied, articulating my desires aloud like I always do. I was the outgoing one, the one that said what either of us couldn't or wouldn't say. Bernd was the quiet one, the reserved one. And together, we made the perfect team. I watched him walk out of the house, my other half leaving me till much later. As soon as the door shut in my face. I segued into my part of the world. Which is why I was startled when the door opened. I didn't know who I was expecting. I certainly wasn't expecting anyone. But I was certainly surprised when I saw Bernd walk in. He had forgotten a trowel or one of his gardening tools, he said. Later I would realize that this was one of the best things that ever happened that day. If he hadn't come in, if he hadn't forgotten whatever tool that he claimed that he forgot, I would have been left alone, stranded, abandoned, an unfit opponent for the people that came after.

He was still searching for whatever he had left behind when the knocks shattered the morning silence of our home.

"Another visitor?" My look said it as though I hadn't confirmed that Bernd was the visitor. But would you blame me? I wasn't used to such interruptions in my day. Before we gathered our thoughts, the sounds of another knock shattered the ambiance of our little home with an urgency that bordered on rudeness. "Who is that?" we both chorused, our eyes fixed on the door, our feet switching between moving and staying in place. Should we go get the door, or should we not? In the backs of our minds, we knew that there was something wrong, something ominous, that the knocks were not those of a

friend. My mind raced like a horse with fire on its tail. The memories of the previous week scurried through. Bernd and I had talked about it. About the gay couple who no one had been able to reach. Most people claimed that they saw them step out of the party, I didn't. But that was the last anyone saw and heard about them. Did this knock have anything to do with them? Nothing could answer this question, nothing could provide the solution to this problem. Yet again, my mind moved to the next option, our friends.

None of our friends would knock, at least not at this time. We ruled out neighbors; they wouldn't be so rude. Because the knock was rude, not just rude, it was demeaning. It felt as though the knocker or whoever was behind the door needed entry the way a drowning man needs air.

Midway to the door, Bernd breezed past me.

Ana wished that she didn't have to look up, but she did, and as she did, she left her finger on the last line, the exact spot she had last read. A creature of habit, just like anyone, the ray of sun which cast its almost invisible glow into the room to signal someone's entry was the reason. She had hoped that she would see Andre. He was supposed to have been at work at that time, but he wasn't. He was as punctual as a working clock. But he wasn't in his usual spot when she arrived.

She had gotten an engaged tone when she dialed his number, and she had hoped that he would call her back as he always did. To her, Andre was that sort of friend, the one that she knew she could call at any time, for any reason. And it was the same with her. And if she wasn't so subsumed in the world that the diary had led her into, she would have realized how much she missed him, how much she had missed his giggles, his loaded glances, and their banters.

Neither of the people who walked in was him. Not the young man with the oversized biker's jacket and dark, slicked-back hair who wore sunglasses indoors. And certainly not the girl with a full head of hair and too-shiny lip gloss who walks on the balls of her feet. She did a quick sweep of the room as the new entrants settled, and before she could do anything else, her attention was arrested. Like someone being sucked into the quicksand, she found herself being pulled back to the diary. If it was interesting before, at that moment, it was much more. The perfect word to describe it would be arresting. She was arrested, hooked, transfixed... yes, subsumed.

We both knew that there was trouble when Bernd's question was left unanswered. My neck tightened and something coiled in my belly at the realization that whatever and whoever was behind our door was danger. Even the air in our room changed; it became charged and heavy.

Instead of an answer, the knock rang out again, louder but shorter. Two loud raps that we interpreted to mean, "this is your last warning; don't keep us waiting." As soon as Bernd's eyes met mine after he turned, I nodded to his unuttered question, asking me if he should go on.

He turned the key in the lock, slid the bolt away, and as he did all of this, it felt as though the same things were happening inside me.

I may forget everything about this day, but I certainly won't forget what happened next; when the door swung open.

At the doorway were four men with faces as cold as a winter night. Even a child would know who they were. Dressed in the outfit of the state police, the four of them, led by a mustachioed leader with gleaming boots and well-starched uniform. I would have known, even without being told that he was the leader. With the way they knocked, I had expected them to storm in, eyes and guns blazing, voice booming and spewing instructions.

I have heard too many stories about their visits for me not to have this fear lodged in my chest like a heavy stone. Who lived in East Berlin and hasn't also heard if not experienced the same thing? The empty building next door was a cautionary tale of a neighbor abducted by the secret police. The hushed whispers that are passed around when friends or family members suddenly go missing. We all have been affected. We all feared.

But they didn't storm in brusquely. Instead, they arranged themselves at the doorway as though they were on parade while the leader asked in a voice that was as thick as his face. If the mood were lighter, if it was another place and another time, I would have laughed at the way his mustache moved as though it had a life of its own. But I couldn't. I was frozen with fear, a fear so real that I was shivering, my chest felt as though something hard and cold had tightened around it, and my heart dropped to my feet.

"Is this the House of Bernd and Gabriella Meyer?" the leading officer's voice erupted, and for a while, it appeared that his voice was thunder and his eyes lightening and the tears that ran all over my body, torrents.

I knew that the question was directed at Bernd. After all, the four pairs of eyes were fixated on him, pointed in his direction. But I found my head nodding. "Yes, it is," Bernd responded, and even if his voice sounded steady, I could still hear the almost inaudible waver in it. And it was this that reminded me of what I heard about courage, about it not being the absence of fear but confidence in the presence of fear.

Butterflies fluttered in my belly as I watched Bernd. While I was shaking, he was standing still in that moment, and I fell in love again. Nothing is as attractive as a courageous man.

The room smelled of the remnants of our breakfast, dust, and the scent of strangers. It reminded me of something nice and un-nice.

The leader produced a piece of paper that was handed to him by one of the stone-faced minions behind him and shoved it under Bernd's nose like someone pushing a bowl of food toward a feral dog.

"We have been instructed to search this facility," he said, and before Bernd's nod was complete, he motioned to the three others to step into the building to invade our space. The message was clear, they weren't here on a courtesy visit. They weren't waiting for our response.

My body tensed like the muscles on the arm of an archer as I expected the moment to turn into something else. My heart slammed hard in my chest, so loud that I feared that everyone in the room would hear the flurried sound. I saw the same tension in Bernd's body as the four stepped into the house. He walked toward me, his eyes locked with mine, his hand reaching for me.

"First, we have a few questions for you," the leader said midstride, his voice cool but cold, and it made me imagine the feeling of a bayonet placed beside my neck.

"Her?" Bernd asked. His voice was broken and distorted like shattered glass. I saw his features darken with fear.

The leader nodded. If he felt like he was being questioned, he didn't indicate it. He had acted almost the same way since the door had opened. I was too shocked to answer; my entire body felt as though I had been taken from a sauna and dumped in the freezing sub-zero snow.

The leader motioned for me to sit on the couch as though I was the guest. This first-time visitor was the perfect host. His voice cool, his manner casual.

I willed my legs that had frozen into pillars and found my way to the couch while Bernd moved as though he was considering joining me. He decided not to but moved to the closest wall to me to lean and watch from a not-too-safe distance.

The soft couch that I sat on felt like a hard rock. I tried not to think of all the lovely times we had on the couch. With the way the leader of the communist police looked at me, I feared that he could see the several bodily fluids that had been shed and washed off the couch.

Unconsciously, I found my hands moving off my lap and to the couch as though to obliterate the stains.

"Be calm... be calm...be calm," I muttered internally. "You have done nothing," I said to the fluttering going on in my head.

"Tell me your name," the leader asked in the same calm tone that he had been using. For a moment, my mind strayed. I wondered if the leader ever smiled, if he had a lover, if he was married, and what his life outside the uniform was like. I wondered what he thought about me, about us.

He cleared his throat, and my mind was redirected to the question that I was asked.

"But you know my name. You know our names. You have it in that warrant that you tucked into the pocket of your starched uniform," I muttered internally, but externally I answered.

"Gabriella... My name is Gabriella." I answered with the most confident voice that I could muster. Yet, despite all of my confidence, I could still hear the fluttering in my voice, the faltering as though strings were plucked by an unsure hand. I tried to hold his gaze, tried to do everything to appear as calm as he was, as unafraid as I would love to be, but I couldn't, so I let my eyes rest on his

chin, his well-shaved chin that I imagined would feel smooth when touched.

His eyes followed me like a man's shadow. He nodded as though what he asked me was a test, and what I responded was the correct answer.

Around me, the room, our home, felt like a matchbox, too small, too dark, in spite of the late-morning sunshine that shone through the windows. His other men were as cool as he was, if I chose to ignore their cold looks and their wandering gaze. They stood like men waiting for instruction, like the keys of a trumpet waiting to be pressed.

Something shifted within me at the nod of his head. In that moment, I couldn't tell if it was relief that I had answered the question or if it was fear that the next question wouldn't be as easy as this one. Outwardly, I kept the best poker face that I could assemble, and I hoped that it showed little or nothing of the fear that I felt inside of me.

"So, what is it that you do?" the leader with the name Henrich stitched on his pocket asked me in a voice that cracked like a whip. It was then that I realized that this was no random visit. Not that I had assumed that it was one before, but I hadn't thought that their visit would have been related to work, to what we do.

Ana reached for her water bottle. Her tongue had been begging for cool relief for a long time. The diary had been too engaging, the events too enthralling. She had found it so hard to pull away, to make way for any other activity. Andre hadn't come or called back, and she was beginning to feel worried. She decided to wait, partly because she wasn't someone prone to panicking and also because she didn't want anything to distract her from the pages in the diary. Like it had always been since she picked up the diary and started her odyssey into the sultry and salacious lives of Gabriella and Bernd. She took time to imagine what they were feeling, how it felt in that moment. Already her heart was racing, beating a staccato beneath her chest. Apart from a few pages before the one that she was in, the diary had been explicit; it had been vivid with details. She had ignored those pages after trying unsuccessfully to make sense of the meaning. Perhaps those pages talked about the missing gay couple or that someone had reported them to the police. She waved her thoughts away with the casualness of someone chasing away a fly and returned her attention to the diary. She felt a sort of kinship with Gabriella. And she hoped that whatever was about to happen would go in her favor.

At first, I thought that I hadn't heard properly, which is why his questions were rewarded with silence.

"I teach people how to make crazy, mad, intense love. I sell amazing sex toys that spice up the sex lives of the people in this part of Berlin."

Those were the words that I wanted to say. For those were the truth about what I did. But I didn't. I couldn't. Even without seeing Bernd, I could hear the sound of his feet scraping the floor as though he was squashing some insect of some sort. I knew that there were no insects in our house. I was too clean for that, and I ensured that the house was too clean for them. What was Bernd doing? I asked myself. Was he giving me a sign, or was he merely moving his leg? There was no way I would know, but I knew that he would not want me to tell the truth. I couldn't tell the truth. The truth was a crime, and the punishment for such a crime was disappearance. At least, that is what we knew happened to the others who experienced a similar fate.

"I do not work," I replied. Yet again, the seat felt like stone beneath me; rivulets of sweat rolled off my body like droplets of rain on a leaf after a heavy downpour. Even as the words left my mouth, I could tell that it wasn't entirely believable.

"I am, we are living on my inheritance," I answered, giving my earlier answer a second leg for stability.

Like a rumple, like a kink, I felt the first change in the officer's face. Whatever information he had, whoever had spoken to him or to his superiors, must have told him something else. His face tightened into a frown.

"That is incorrect," he answered, his voice congealed with exasperation as he leaned into the couch.

I saw the other three agents each move but remain at the same spot as though awaiting a prompt from him, like hunting dogs waiting for the hunter's whistle. The couch protested against his weight. A noise that was too loud in the too-quiet room that our living room had become.

"What is incorrect?" I asked. My brows were chiseled with a crippling worry, my body drenched with dripping sweat. How could he accuse me in my house? I queried him in my thoughts. I was red hot with anger. But externally, I waited. I was quiet. My body tensed as I waited for his response, as I awaited the sign that would show that he knew something that he shouldn't have known.

"I have it on good authority that you are involved in something illegal," he responded.

The word "illegal" hung in the air, and everyone looked around the room. I did, too, and so did the other police, looking from wall to wall; even Bernd did. The head who had been asking me the questions looked at the row of shelves that rested on the wall as though the "illegal" things that he mentioned were there.

"I have no idea what you are talking about," I answered. My confidence soaring like an eagle coasting in the clouds. I didn't know if Bernd could sense what I could, but I suddenly knew that they knew nothing. Whichever story they knew, whichever allegation that they had made about or against us, would only stand when they had evidence.

And because I knew that there was no evidence in the house, I felt the loosening in my chest. A week ago, after we confirmed that the gay couple could have been picked up by police, we found us a Soviet boy who charged us a lot. Bernd protested, but I insisted. His charge was worth the risk he was eliminating for us, I told him. So, I paid him to help dispose of all the sex toys. We would get them when the danger had passed, we concluded. And it was because of this that I felt a joy incomparable even with the stone-faced agents in the room.

"So, do you have any document to prove your claim?" He asked me, his face still unreadable, but I could sense something akin to mockery in his voice.

"Of course," I answered, and I motioned to the shelf. He nodded his approval, and I moved my legs, heavy as rocks, to the shelf.

I felt his eyes following me, not just his but the other four pairs in the room, and instead of a crippling sense of self-consciousness that I usually feel when strangers are *watching me, I felt an anxiety, an apprehension. I wanted more than anything for the day to be over, for the moment to pass as fast as possible, and I could tell that it was Bernd's desire also. I couldn't tell if it was the same desire of the police. At the drawer, I knew just where to look, and in less than a minute, I had the documents in my hands. The papers felt too brittle as I carried them back to my seat.*

"Here they are," I said in my most confident voice as the familiarity of my couch welcomed my body. I waited to be seated before handing them to him as a form of silent protest of our home invasion.

He received the sheaf of papers and peered at them as though the words were too tiny. I watched and waited, expecting him to tell me that he had seen what I presented to him, expecting him to tell us that they were done and ready to go.

He took longer than necessary, flipping from page to page, his head moving like a judge perusing through documentary evidence or a doctor reading a medical report.

"It is there … all you need is right there." I challenged him internally. Externally, I folded my hands in my lap, and my gaze was daggers being shot at him. After a while, a few moments that extended to an eternity, I began to fear that I had given him the wrong document.

He arranged the documents carefully as though they were fragile things that would break if he treated them otherwise.

And as I watched him, he snapped his fingers like some leader of an orchestra, and the men that had been waiting sprang into action.

The other parts of the shelf were opened and emptied. As we protested, the same thing went on in our bedroom, in our kitchen, in every room. When they finally left, our entire house felt like a place that a tornado and a volcano had been through.

After the first minutes of their departure, even to days after, Bernd and I lived in mortal fear. Every knock sounded in our hearts, and every stranger that walked behind us on the road felt like the secret police. Bernd suggested that we move, and I agreed if not for what halted our plans. Another knock on our door one warm evening. It wasn't loud, but the fear that lodged in our chests still made us jump. When the door swung open, we found a quivering woman there.

Shivering and close to tears, she dropped the bombshell as soon as we beckoned her in. "How do I sustain my marriage?" she blurted out. "My husband rarely touches me," she added in a voice that broke my heart and reduced our suspicion. "I don't believe that he loves me anymore, and the only reason I'm with him, the *only reason I'm still staying with him, is because of our children." I counseled her like I had done with many before her. Her husband still loved her, I assured her, but probably she is the one who isn't as attractive as she always was. I gave her some things to use. A perfume to wear before she got into bed, a negligee to wear in bed, and some toys to liven up their dying flame of love. Her coming changed everything for us, for me especially. Many would suffer if we left, relationships would shatter without us. The smile on her face did it for me. I would stay. "We should stay," I said to Bernd as soon as the door slammed shut against her.*

"We will," Bernd said, and as though he had been thinking about it, he added, "We really shouldn't have kids."

"We shouldn't," I agreed. This has been our decision since I started advising couples. From what I observed, the coming of kids always changed couples, and we both didn't want to change. I could tell that Bernd didn't want anything to stop him from kissing me the way he did after I said that, and I didn't want anything also to stop me from feeling the way I was feeling at that moment. Not crying babies or grumpy teens. Nothing.

5: A GOOD TIME

It had been eating her up, gnawing at her insides like a cancer, like a tapeworm in her gut. She had asked herself the question like a prosecutor examining a witness. She had done it so much, so often, that she had even found herself muttering it aloud like a mantra of some sort. Till it almost embarrassed her in public.

She had tried to visualize it as she did with all the characters in the books she read. Sansa Stark, in her head, before she watched the show, was pretty and innocent as the writer had depicted in *Game of Thrones*. Perhaps prettier than the actress that eventually played her. Robert Langdon was like a typical English professor in her imagination. In her head, she had imagined him dressed in Harris tweed and his face bearing a contemplative look like Dan Brown had depicted in his book *Inferno*. The one in the movie was better looking.

But what did Gabriella and Bernd look like? She had a clue to this because of the pictures that she saw in the pile. She knew what they looked like with the help of the black and white photos that she had picked up alongside the diary.

How was East Berlin in the 1980s? This also was almost solved with the images that she gleaned from the grainy pictures and from the internet.

But the most important question remained unanswered. *How was sex, and the conditions regarding sex, thought of in those times?* This was what she needed to know. Ana knew that she shouldn't be bothered, but she was.

That was how her mind worked. Once it set out on a path, it wouldn't settle till it reached its destination. It always reminded her of a quote that hung inside a frame on one of the walls of the library. *When the mind of a man is expanded by an idea, it can never return to its normal shape again.*

That was how her mind was, a stretched string, a roaming thing. It had been that way since she began reading the diary.

To answer that question. To satisfy that curiosity of hers. She did what anyone in her generation would. She searched the internet. She typed question after question, looking for the elusive answer.

What did the communist police do to sexual deviants in East Berlin?

Sex in East Berlin in the 1980s

Queer sex in East Berlin

Some of her searches were sensible, others weren't. And the search engine was quick to remind with the response.

It looks like there aren't many great matches for your search.

Try using words that might appear on the page you're looking for.

She let her imagination do what imaginations do. For a while, the products of her imagination made sense. But it was only for a while. It soon fell apart because it didn't feel solid or believable for her. She needed something solid, not a third person's point of view like most of the results she got from the internet. It was then she remembered her grandmother or Oma (German for granny), as Ana often called her. Oma should have the sort of answers that she was looking for. She decided that she would ask her.

As she descended the stairs that morning, it was the same thought that occupied her mind. Her grandmother has been doing what she loved.

Oma's at it again, Ana mused thoughtfully as her senses were assailed.

She could tell from the delicious smells that hung in the air. The palate-watering scent of freshly baked bread mixed with an assortment of piquant fish, peas, and potatoes.

She saw in the curl of her lips and the crows' feet at the corners of her emerald eyes when she met her glance. She could hear it in the rhythm of the song she hummed as she arranged the plates on the table. She even expected to hear her say her favorite words. *Cooking is an art of love. You only cook for those you love.* Her grandmother was like that. And she knew where her father had gotten his knack for repetition from. It definitely was from her. Her stomach growled in acknowledgment of the mélange of scents that filled the room, but the accompanying appetite that often followed such growl was missing.

"Look who came early for breakfast this morning," her grandmother surprised her by saying something else as Ana's foot settled into the plush carpet at the bottom of the stairs. Ana pretended not to notice the table set for four. It was another thing her grandmother did, setting the table for four even if her parents were not around. She would tell her, if she asked, that they could come home at any time. Even if they both knew that her parents wouldn't come in that day or even that week. *Perhaps it is one of the things that came with old age, being stuck with such patterns,* Ana thought.

"Hi, Oma," she said as she covered the distance between her and Flora. She hugged her as she always did from when she was a little girl, wrapping her hands around her and burying her face in her neck. The scent of the breakfast that hung on her clothes, combined with her natural scent of home and warmth, wafted into her nostrils as she pressed her lips against Oma's wrinkly face. She inhaled the scent greedily, again, as she always does.

"Is that how you will greet your oma?" her grandmother asked with a lifted eyebrow as she sensed that something was up with Ana. Ana could tell that it was because of the absence of a smile and the lack of chirpiness in her voice.

Arms that were too strong for her age released *Oma* from the embrace.

"I'm sorry, Oma," she quipped as she settled into her place at the end of the table. "I just have stuff on my mind that I have been trying to figure out," Ana said as her eyes met with Oma's again.

"Why not tell me... or is it something that your oma cannot figure out?" she said as she brought the bread to the table. Her eyes gleaming with excitement and expectation. Her grandmother said the words with a hint of the sardonic in them. Years ago, before Ana knew about encyclopedias and the internet, her grandmother used to be her go-to walking encyclopedia. It was she that Ana asked about everything that children of her age asked. It was from her that she learned about sex, dragons, God. But as Ana grew, that part of their relationship petered out, especially when Ana discovered the internet. But Oma never forgot. As a matter of fact, she missed it, and she always used any opportunity to remind her of what they once shared.

"Do you know anything about the sex in East Berlin during the 80s?" Ana blurted out with the swiftness of someone who couldn't wait to ask the question.

It was the smile on her grandmother's face that made her realize that her question may have been misleading.

"Oh, my little angel has found herself someone from East Berlin." Her blue eyes misted and shined at her granddaughter with unsuppressed joy. Her wrinkly hands clapped together underneath her jaw as though she had just discovered something strange.

What have I just said? Ana queried herself internally, rolling her eyes externally and smacking her head gently.

"That's not what I meant," she said, stretching her hand across the table to her grandmother's hands, which were now curled over a napkin. The way her grandmother cocked her head in confusion further worried her.

How do I fix this? she pondered as she searched for the right words, the right way to phrase the question.

"What I meant is that I would like to know how things were during those times since you might have known people who lived in the era?" Ana rambled. She searched her grandmother's face for signs of comprehension. Her grandmother had always been someone with a sound mind for a woman her age, so she knew if she didn't understand her question, it was because she didn't ask the right question.

So, when she saw the look of understanding on her grandmother's face, she knew that her grandmother had finally understood the question. Ana sat back in her chair, taking the pose of someone ready to drink in the lessons that she knew she would definitely get from Flora.

"This is what I know about sex during those times," her grandmother said as she began. Her eyes were lit with the excitement of someone who had found something that she had longed for, for a long time.

As she dug into the breakfast, she listened as her grandmother took her through the journey of what she knew about those times. Just as she thought, the internet's version was different from her grandmother's version. Stories Flora told are often better, even if they were dramatized in her own signature way, designed to leave no one indifferent.

It surprised her how much her grandmother knew. Yet she wasn't so surprised because Flora was like that. Her father still teased her grandmother with the nickname "walking dictionary." There was hardly anything she didn't know. And Ana remembered those growing-up moments fondly as she sat at that table, her food growing cold, her mind getting blown.

As Oma spoke, the spaces that before were vacant began to fill up. A part of Ana felt exhilarated about the knowledge that she now had; however, she felt a crippling sadness descend on her as she finally began to understand what Gabriella and her husband may have felt during those times. The fear that would have influenced every action they took. The dread that would have colored their lives, especially after the visit of the communist police. The rest of the breakfast became more like a routine. The savory taste of the food was lost. But she knew that she still had to eat because her grandmother still treated her as a little child, especially regarding matters like that. She would order her to finish her leftovers, to fill up the bones that were jutting out in her body. So, she did. As Ana left the table, she knew that her grandmother still thought that she had fallen in love with an East Berliner. But since she didn't mention it, she let her thoughts be.

But in Ana's head, a new thought also had formed.

Theo

She had wanted to have sex with Theo. She had even told Andre. It would have happened that Sunday after the ice cream date. Ana wanted to ask Theo to come with her. She was hoping that he would tell her to come back home with him. Especially with all the fun they had. The touching of each other's arms, the tasting of each other's ice cream, the laughter that rumbled through their bellies, the ease with which they spoke. Everything was perfect. Even the weather. But she couldn't ask him because of a crippling fear that froze the words in her chest each time she wanted to say it. She couldn't tell if it was shyness or fear. The fear of refusal. The fear that he would say 'no' to her. Maybe it was both.

So, she decided to call him, and hopefully tell him what she should have told him then. Or maybe just check up on him.

It was exactly what she did as soon as she cleared the table. It was a Saturday, and with no work to be done at the library, Ana knew that the entire day stretched out ahead of her, filled with no activities.

He picked up on the first ring as though he had been waiting for her call. After the initial pleasantries were exchanged, Ana asked what he had been up to and why she hadn't seen him in a while. As they spoke, she imagined Andre laughing at her, teasing her when she tells him how she missed conversing with Theo. It was what he always did whenever she told him about them. "I thought you said you didn't want someone back then," he would always tease.

Theo told her that he was on break and in search of a place to work. It finally made sense to her, his absence and all. Unasked, he told her of the places that he had applied to, the places that had promised to give him a callback. As they were speaking, Ana remembered a vacancy available at the library. It had been posted physically on the notice board that was in the staff room and also digitally on the staff's WhatsApp group. She wanted to mention it, but she converted it into a sneeze.

She was a few moments away from telling him, but she suddenly realized how awkward it would be working with someone she liked. So, she decided against it. She was glad he didn't suspect that her sneeze was not really a sneeze. She felt guilt settle over her.

The best thing she could do to compensate for the guilt that gnawed at her was to look out for other opportunities for him. That's what she would do. She made a mental note to do just that.

Just before the call ended, Theo told her about a place that he would like her to see. "Let's have breakfast together today," he said. "I know this place that you would love to see."

Even with her belly brimming with her grandmother's food, the offer was too grand to refuse, too enticing to turn down. She wanted to not just see the place that Theo thought would be fascinating to her but also to spend time with him. No matter how unbelievable it sounded, she could tell that she missed him. And from the way his voice sounded on the phone, she could tell that the feeling was indeed mutual.

"Sure. Send me the address, and I will be right there," she said excitedly into the phone. The thrill of seeing him slowly replaced the guilt that had settled on her shoulders before.

The address came via text message immediately, and with a few clicks, Ana was able to check where the location was. Not too far. It was twenty minutes away from the house. As soon as the call was over. Ana picked up her bag, and with a breezy, "I will be right back, Oma," she stepped out of the house into the warm summer weather.

The sky was golden, and a warm breeze was singing through the trees that lined the streets. It caressed her face and skin. Everywhere she looked was filled with bright colors—ladies in floral sundresses, men in shorts and gaudy T-shirts. It was one of the reasons why she loved summer.

Throughout the twenty-minute trip, Ana's thoughts swung between two points like a displaced pendulum. The first was her blossoming friendship with Theo, and the other was the insight into the lives of Gabriella and Bernd. They both fascinated her in different ways. She chose to be candid with herself, which is a trait that she picked up from her mother. She hadn't imagined that she and Theo would grow so close, close enough that they would spend time together having meals, that she would feel excited spending time with him. But it had happened, it was happening, and it fascinated her. But she couldn't tell if he would be the answer to her parents' desire, the knight that saved her from spinsterhood and singleness. Time would tell, she concluded. As usual, she also thought about Gabriella and Bernd's life. It was different now; things were different in her head. If before the picture of their lives in her head was colorless, now it was streaked with colors, thanks to her grandmother's version of events.

Unconsciously, she reached out for the diary to continue from where she stopped, to resume the journey that had been suspended, but as her hand landed on her small tote, she remembered that she had left it in her room. Moments later, the cab slowed in front of an arcane-looking building. Even before the cab driver spoke, she knew that she had arrived at the location.

The building was like any of the buildings in the area if she chose to ignore the freshly painted doors and windows or the signage that announced its name to passersby or patrons like her.

The Zur Letzten Instanz was one of the oldest, if not the oldest, restaurants in East Berlin, with a specialty breakfast menu. From her brief perusal on Trip Advisor, she had seen the features that stood out. The courthouse theme, the array of lip-smacking delicacies. As she took tentative steps to the front of the four-hundred-year-old edifice, something stirred within her. She could tell that she hadn't been here before. She was more of a burger and coke person, and with the sort of memory that she had, she knew that there was no way that she wouldn't have known if she had come here either as a child or an adult. She couldn't tell what it was that made this restaurant that occupied two stories of the four-storied edifice seem eerily familiar. She stopped as soon as she got to the doorstep and took it all in. If anyone had seen her staring, they would have thought she was some tourist or an architecture lover.

Her eyes traveled from the first floor to the last. She counted the windows without meaning to. Each floor had a total of three long windows, like most of the houses in the area, like most German houses of that age. She knew enough about architecture, as much as a bibliophile like her could know. The predominant architecture in most German regions, including this particular area, was Bauhaus style. Staatliches Bauhaus was a school of design that was established in nineteenth-century Germany as a school of fine arts, design, and architecture, she had read. The judicious use of glass, concrete, and steel, all adorned with green. Bauhaus architecture was notable for the use of primary colors, style and simplicity were the identifying factors of a Bauhaus-style house. And that is what she noticed in this particular building. But it wasn't the architecture that had her standing and staring. It was something else. Perhaps she had driven past here before, perhaps her eyes had picked up the building, and her mind had stored it in her subconscious. She knew the expression that closely described what she felt. Déjà vu. But apart from the façade of the building, the electric lamps that were jutting out of the walls, the linden and oak trees that formed a natural canopy over the road in front of the building, etc. It all looked like somewhere out of her past.

Ana could tell that she had never been to that part of town, but it looked oddly similar to somewhere she had seen recently. She was still in this daze when an arm slipped underneath hers. She juddered as though a bucket filled with cold water had been poured over her. She turned to see Theo's smiling face. Her racing heart slowed immediately like a car that had suddenly applied its brakes.

"I've been calling you for ages," he said. His topaz eyes were searching her face for a sign that she was alright.

For a moment, Ana's mouth turned to dust, and her tongue felt like something tangled and bound. She couldn't reply, nor could she say, "Hi." For a while, the silence that followed seemed thick like a heavy blanket. And she could only look from the building to Theo as if she was looking for the elusive answers in his face.

"I'm sorry, Theo," she blurted when she finally came to herself. Blood rushed to her cheek and neck in embarrassment as she realized she had been acting like someone caught in a daze.

"I am sometimes like this," Ana lied, and she could see the furrow of confusion on Theo's face. But that was all she could say, all the words that she could manage to bandy as an excuse for her faux pas.

She hugged him as though to distract him from whatever thoughts were simmering within him. But she also did it to take her mind away from the persistent memory that the building had dug out from her head.

"It's fine," he whispered into her hair and hugged her harder. "I just hope that *you* are fine?" he asked in a voice laden with concern.

A wave of warmth seeped into Ana like spilled oil.

"I am...I actually am," Ana replied. "Can we go in now?" she said as they pulled away from each other. Whatever this was, she concluded, she would figure it out later.

"After you," Theo said as he pushed the door open. She smiled at his chivalry, at his gentlemanliness. Oma would like him if Ana told her about him. She was sure about this. She was as old school as old school could be, and she was always complaining about how Ana's generation no longer cared about things like that.

"I wonder if your children will know how to treat ladies or act as gentlemen?" she would often say to Ana as though Ana already had children of her own.

As soon as they entered the restaurant, the scent of the mouth-watering delicacies wafted into their nostrils and washed over them like the spray of sea waves. Ana had thought that she would not eat anything. After all, she had just stuffed herself with her grandmother's food. She had left nothing, not even a crumb on her plate. And she had felt as full as a stuffed burger. But she found her eyes drawn to the pastries on display, and her mouth salivated. She couldn't tell if it was because she was in the café or because somehow her fullness had dissipated in the short time it took her to get there.

"This place smells good," she quipped as she waited for him to lead the way. They settled in seats not far from the entrance but private enough so that they wouldn't be the spectacle for everyone who came in. Ana preferred looking at people and not people looking at her. It irritated her, so she was glad he had chosen a perfect table.

"So, how have you been?" Theo asked.

"Very good ...very good," Ana replied, her attention taken by the menu in her hands. She was glad that she finally had something that took her mind away from the déjà vu kind of feeling.

"What about you?" she asked, finally looking up. The words of her grandmother sounded so loud in her ears, as though she was behind her. *"It is rude to do something else when someone is talking to you."*

"Oh, you know what I have been up to," he said with the knowing smile of someone who tells all the happenings in their lives to their friends. He rubbed his thumb and index finger together as if flipping through a book or counting money. Ana noticed that he had been doing that since he sat down, and she wondered if that was a nervous habit of his, just like the way her father always unconsciously ran his hands through his beard or her grandmother cleaning what she has already cleaned.

"So, what will you have?" he asked as he picked up his copy of the menu from the table.

"I think I will start with a drink," Ana said. Summer might be great, but it came with its heat and the attentive need to constantly hydrate. If Ana needed a reason to hate summer, it was this. But it wasn't reason enough.

"I will have this combo of apple-carrot-orange juice. The apfel-karotten-orangensaft," she said. "If the scents wafting over here is anything to be trusted, I think I would love to try the Maultaschen. With minced meat." Ana added.

"Trust me, you will enjoy it. All the food here is delicious," Theo replied with a self-assured response. Later, Ana will realize that he had a good enough reason for that response.

They placed their order as soon as the server, a girl with a too-tight bun and a too-white shirt, came around. Ana would have told her how pretty she was, but she decided against it.

When the server left their table, Ana's mind returned to the same thought, *What is it about this place that seems so familiar?* she asked herself again. But the answer simply eluded her and remained on the fringes of her mind.

They dug into their lunch as soon as it arrived, and just as Ana had hoped, the meal was as delicious as the scent.

While they ate, Theo told her that he had started to read a book, and he hoped that it would be the first book that he would ever finish. Ana listened and tried to add the complimentary comments that she knew would make the conversation continue uninhibited, but her mind was elsewhere. Where had she seen this building before?

Suddenly, like an epiphany of some sort, the answer came to her.

Immediately, she pulled a picture from her bag, and staring right at her were images of the interior and exterior of the building. For a moment, she was petrified; it felt as though her blood had curdled within her; it felt as though her bones had frozen, as though her entire body was weighed down with bricks.

There, in the picture, was Gabriella and her husband posing in front of the same breakfast café where she and Theo were. Minutes before, Theo had excused himself to go use the restroom, and with only the remnants of their lunches and an empty seat in front of her, she bolted outside to confirm her discovery. There was no denying that it was the same place, she realized as she looked from picture to present reality. Her arms filled up with goose pimples, and her heart slammed furiously against her chest. Excitement and nervousness coursed through her blood. And she soon felt her hand shaking as though she had suddenly seen their ghosts appear in front of her. She couldn't tell how long she had been there, or how ashen she looked, or how enraptured she was.

It wasn't until she felt Theo's hand on the small of her back and his voice asking if the picture that she held in her hands was a picture of her grandparents. It was that comment that untangled her, that broke her from the spell.

With her eyes still on the picture, she laughed it off as the shock of her discovery slowly washed off her. "Talking about grandparents," she said as she turned to face him. Her hand sliding the picture into her bag. "I think it's time you met my actual grandmother. Would you come home with me?" she asked him.

"Of course I will," Theo replied, his eyes shining with excitement at the unexpected offer. For a while, they stood at the entrance, not moving. It felt as though they were each taking in the sights differently.

Theo broke the silence. "I hope you enjoyed the meal."

"Oh yes, I did," Ana said as she casually touched his shoulder, her face glowing with the radiance of a thousand suns.

"I knew that you would...this is one of the places that I trust most in Berlin," he said as his hands slid into his pockets. "I have been coming here since I was a kid," he added casually, but the words got Ana's attention.

"Since when you were a kid?" she asked with genuine alarm. Her mind began to reel with questions. *This must have been why he had been so sure about their food*, Ana pondered. It made sense to her at that moment.

"Yes," he answered, with a surprised look of his own. "Did you know that this is one of the oldest cafés in Berlin?" he asked her with the enthusiasm of someone who knew that she didn't and wouldn't mind sharing it.

"No, I didn't," she answered. Ana could feel question after question jostle within her. So, she chose one. "Tell me about it; tell me everything you know about this place." Her hands made a sweep of the building in front of them.

And as they stood there, Theo with his hands in his pockets and his face lit up with excitement, and Ana with her bag slung over one arm and her head filled with questions. She listened as he gave her a rough up-to-date history of the café. And just as he was finishing, he said something that further set the thoughts in Ana's head into another flurried state.

"I know the owner. We talk often," Theo said with the casualness that Ana was slowly getting used to.

"Let's go check in on him," she said. Without a word, he headed back into the café. Ana trudged after him, her body quaking with excitement. Unconsciously, her hand dropped to her bag. She knew that regardless of how rude it would seem, she would definitely ask about Gabriella and Bernd.

The office they went to was located at the back of the café. Through the glass door, Ana saw a white-haired man with the tanned skin of someone with a love for the outdoors whose name she later knew was Jens Emery. The man rose to greet Theo as soon as he saw him.

If Ana disbelieved Theo's tale, the cordial salutation was enough proof to change her mind.

After the warm embrace and the pleasantries that followed, Theo introduced Ana as his special friend, and before she realized what was happening, Jens had pulled her into a warm embrace of her own. He beckoned them to sit, despite Theo's protest that he just came to say hello to him. Just like her grandmother would do, Jens soon ignored Theo and focused on her, showering her with questions. They were the sort of questions any elderly person like him would ask—questions about work, her parents, and if she had enjoyed the meal.

Ana realized that she may never get a better chance to find out about Gabriella, so she pulled out the picture and showed it to Jens.

"Do you happen to know these people?" she asked. Jens picked up the picture and peered at it with his bespectacled face.

Her heart thrummed in her chest as a temporary silence breathed between them. *Please know them, please know them*, Ana prayed internally.

"Oh, yes," Jens answered suddenly, and Ana felt her heart drop to her feet. "I remember them," Jens said, and Ana felt her excitement beat loud in her ears.

"You know them?" he asked, leaning in his chair and looking at Ana's face as though trying to find the connection, the relationship between Ana and the couple.

"Not really," Ana replied. She was grateful that Jens hadn't taken offense about her bringing a stranger's picture to him or insisted on knowing his relationship with the couple. Instead, he confirmed that Gabriella and her husband lived close by and visited there often, but their disappearance was a mystery.

"They just stopped coming in," he added in a voice laden with nostalgia and sadness. And for a while, the sadness settled over the room. Ana asked what year they disappeared, and he told them it was early 1988. She felt a fearful twinge within her as though she knew Gabriella and her husband personally, and she tried not to imagine what had happened to them. As they left, Jens told her to promise that she would always come back.

She did. Ana realized that he was the kind of person that couldn't be refused. Theo drove her home, and Jens, not the picture, was the subject of their conversation, even if Ana's thoughts were only about Gabriella, her husband, and the disappearance.

Ana wondered why the relics she found were from other venues, not this one. She managed to stay in the conversation, but her mind was a cluttered closet, a circuit box filled with tangled wires. Despite the new answers, she still had more questions. Perhaps even more questions than she had before she met Jens.

It was when they pulled up in front of her house that she realized what she had done. The gravity of her spur-of-the-moment action stared her right in the face. She had actually brought a man to the house, but it was too late to do anything. So, she braced herself, and she ushered Theo into the house that was filled with the aroma of cooking.

She made the introductions to her wide-eyed grandmother. "Oma, meet my friend. His name is Theo. Theo, meet my oma. Her name is Flora."

Like Jens did to her, her grandmother, in between attending to her steaming pots and pans, hijacked Theo from her.

Seeing that chance, Ana snuck up to her room to continue her findings. She heard her plying him with questions as she ascended the stairs. And she felt both pity and relief of some sort. Pity because she knew how endless her grandmother's questions were, and relief because she would have the time that she needed to read the diary.

On getting to her room, Ana discovered that the diary was not where she left it. In its place was emptiness. She searched for it, flinging clothes, upturning furniture as though what she was looking for was a needle and not a book. She finally breathed a breath of relief when she found it on her table. And it was then she concluded that the change in location meant one thing, Flora; her grandmother had probably read it. Angry and exhausted from the search, Ana stormed down the stairs, whining and pining about Flora touching her stuff.

Flora explained that she had only moved it when she was cleaning the room. It sounded probable but unbelievable to Ana. And so, forgetting herself, she found herself whining like she often does when totally pissed. What her grandmother called "bratty moments."

It was in this melee of raised voices and complaints that Theo excused himself and left.

Minutes later, Ana was ensconced in the comfort of her room. The diary securely in front of her, Ana listened to the trill of the phone. As soon as she heard Theo's voice on the line, she uttered the words that had been burning in her throat. "Theo, I'm sorry that you saw all that... I'm sorry that you had to leave that way."

6: THE SEARCH

When Ana was younger, it usually took days before she and Flora eventually talked after disagreements like this. But things were different now. She knew it, and she could sense that Flora did, also.

Yet Ana was still angry. She could still feel the wisps of burnt-out rage curling from the pit of her belly, but that was all. Her anger had reduced, her fury dwindled, and now they were talking as though nothing had happened. Even if she knew that the past disagreement hung between them like a wraith, like the scent of something burning. She knew she had overreacted but was in no mood to apologize. She had apologized to the only person she knew she owed an apology to, Theo.

She understood Flora's obsessive need to clean her environment to ensure that things are spick and span. Anyone who knew Flora knew this about her. But she also knew that cleaning isn't the same thing as searching. Cleaning her room didn't give her the right to go through her stuff. It is possible to do one without the other. She had said this to her several times. They often had similar fights when she was a teen. On those days when she would come back to the house and find her room arranged, only for

Flora to ask her a few days after about a letter that she had seen or an assignment that she had been graded poorly on. At first, she would wonder how Flora had been privy to the information. It then began to make sense after a while. Flora had seen whatever she saw when she arranged her room.

"Your mom and dad said they would be spending an extra week in Paris," Flora blurted, breaking the ice, shattering the silence that had settled over them after her morning greeting. Ana knew what was happening the way she knew the back of her hand. She could tell that Flora was doing that thing she always does whenever she has stuff on her mind—cleaning. Ana could tell that she had already dusted the television twice that morning and had also wiped the center table more than half a dozen times. But she watched her as she still did both. And Ana knew that she would have to break the promise she had made herself on the day of the argument. She would have to shove her ego aside and, like her grandmother always said, "Be the better person." *Why do I have to be the better person today?* she thought angrily.

"Oh, okay... I'm sure that they have their reasons," Ana retorted as she filled up the silence that had settled like a hollow container between them. The presence of her parents always filled her with an ambivalence of some sort. She loved having them around. Their visits were often characterized by the gifts they brought along and mementos from their destinations. Books for her, some clothes, and anything they felt she would like. She often saw these gifts as a bribe of some sort, their lame attempt at compensating her for being unavailable in her life. She also knew that she was no longer that little girl who needed her parents' presence. But it seemed they either didn't know or chose to ignore it. She was satisfied with the unique combination of presence and absence—of them being around and being away. It allowed her to be herself. Isn't that what being alive is? The ability to be oneself all the time? She mused about this that morning.

However, in recent times, their presence hasn't been precisely worthy of being anticipated. The little peace that she enjoyed was due to their absence. If they had been present, she knew she would have been hounded with their demands of getting herself a boyfriend and bringing home a partner as though a boyfriend was like any of the gifts they brought for her during any of the trips.

"Didn't they tell you?" her grandmother said as she looked up from trying to remove a stain that had attained permanent status on the table. Yet again, Ana noticed how focused she was on it as though she hadn't tried removing it unsuccessfully before.

I just have to apologize to her. "No," Ana replied. And she was glad to hear that the coffee grinder had ground the coffee beans completely. It meant that she would be leaving for work soon. The hands of the clock showed that she was on time.

"They didn't tell me," she added as an afterthought as she strode towards the kitchen.

She wondered if Flora didn't know that her parents don't tell her that sort of thing. They just appeared and disappeared like parents do. And recently began giving demands like parents do.

An exhalation was Flora's response to her. So, Ana dropped the steaming cup of coffee on the dining table and walked to where Flora was running the mustard-colored duster over the light sockets like a detective looking for an elusive clue at a crime scene. Only Ana knew that she was no detective and that was no crime scene, and that the place had been cleaned minutes earlier.

Ana hugged her grandmother's shoulders from behind and nuzzled her face in Flora's hair. She felt Flora's body stiffen with surprise.

"Ana," she whispered in the voice of someone amazed at Ana's ambush.

"I am sorry that I misbehaved when Theo was here on Saturday," Ana whispered into Flora's ears. "I was mad that you went through my stuff," Ana continued. And in that moment, she was a five-year-old, a thirteen-year-old, a much younger version of herself.

"You are always mad that I go through your stuff, baby," Flora remarked and pressed Ana closer to her. "I am also sorry for going through your stuff... I really am," Flora added. They both knew she was sorry, yet they each knew she would do it again. They remained like that until Ana realized that her coffee was growing cold and that she might be late if she didn't leave for work.

"I have to go to work now," she said after kissing her grandmother on her cheek. "I'll be back," Ana said as she hurried to grab her coffee.

"Of course. You will be back until Thad, or whatever your friend's name is, steals you from me?" she added in a voice colored with jealousy.

"Oma. His name is Theo, and no one is stealing me from you," Ana responded.

"Your dad said so once," she teased in her usual chirpy voice. And Ana could notice that the air around them had changed. It was freer and lighter. They both were happier.

"Goodbye, Oma." Ana picked up her burgundy bag, sipped from her coffee, and closed the door behind her. As she stepped into the sunshine, she couldn't help but remember how bright the smile on her grandmother's face was and how light she felt.

•••••••

"Oh, my God! Girl, you can't be serious," Andre gasped in his high-pitched voice as quietly as he could. Still, it didn't sound quiet to Ana. His eyes were wide as saucers, one of his hands clamped to his lips while the other curled around Ana's hand. She looked around, first at the door that led to Mr. Novak's office, then at the sprinkling of people busy with their books.

"Shhh," Ana tried to hush him, her index finger across her lips, her eyes rolling into her head. *You just cannot be quiet, Andre*, she thought as she glared at him.

Finally, he quieted and fixed her with the gaze that seemed to say, *please confirm or refute the story*. And she would have stopped or saved their gossip for their break time, but she knew that such would not even be possible. Andre was like a raging fire, and he would certainly badger her or, even worse, guilt trip her if she didn't continue. So, she did.

"That was exactly what happened," Ana whispered with a nod.

"You mean you took Theo home?" he managed to whisper conspiratorially like someone who was inferring something other than what she had told him. And for a minute, she wished she could slap the etched smirk off his face. She had already told him that they didn't do anything. But his look suggested that he didn't believe her.

"You also had a big fight with your granny in his presence?"

She nodded again, knowing he wasn't done yet. *I didn't say a fight.* Ana corrected him internally but nodded externally. She knew that whatever she would have said would have had no effect on Andre. Like an excited electron that moves from one point to another, once excited, Andre only hears whatever he wants, not whatever was said.

"You mean that you also discovered that Gabriella and her lover were living nearby and even visited a restaurant that you went to?" The questions chased after each other in typical Andre fashion. His hands cupped over his mouth, and his eyes widened as though he was the one who had made the discovery. Again, her eyes traveled to the door, hoping to see the form of Mr. Novak with his oversized suit and grumpy look.

"Yes… that is what happened," Ana replied, ignoring the slight irritation crawling like a hundred millipedes in her belly. She hated repetitions, but with Andre, she knew she had to get used to it. Andre was the kind of friend that would make one tell a tale a hundred times the same way, not because he didn't understand it but because he loved the act of talking and gossiping.

She had once told him how he was more of a girl than her. And even if she had meant it as a tease, a sardonic jibe,

Andre had seen it as something else. He considered it a compliment, to which he snapped his fingers and responded gleefully about how he already knew that.

"So how many of us know about the diary now," he asked jealously as he realized that he wasn't an exclusive member of the *diary knowers club*. His voice dropped to a barely audible whisper, and his hand drew invisible circles in the air as though the diary was something round.

"If I choose to omit Theo, who hasn't asked much about it, I would say that it's two," Ana replied, counting the number on her fingers.

"That's me and Flora," he replied in an animated voice that suggested he was excited at her response. He was still an exclusive member. *Three isn't such a crowd, after all.* Ana imagined that this would be the content of his thoughts.

Ana nodded. She still needed to find out if the two people who knew about the diary were the best people that she would have wanted to know about this secret. But they did, and she knew she had to awaken to that reality.

A sound of whispering voices broke out at the corner of the room, prompting them both to look in that direction.

"I'll handle that," Andre volunteered, tucking his shirt into his pants and smacking his lips as though he had just applied invisible lip balm, "but I will be right back," reminding her that the conversation was far from over. And then he sashayed away quietly in his noiseless sneakers.

She shooed him away with the flick of her hand, but her eyes followed him as he walked towards the disturbance. The ghost of a smile formed on her face as she realized how much he reminded her of sweet pain. Something that was so inconvenient yet unforgettable.

If anyone had told her that she would have a friend that was her contemporary, she would have laughed in the person's face. Maybe even told them that it was impossible. She had hung out with older people all her life. Her grandmother's friends were also her friends. At first, they tried sending her away from their midst. It wasn't overt; they often devised one task or the other. "Get us water, fetch food from the kitchen," and anything else that came to mind. But she would often get the things and return to listen to their tales, their reminiscing of their pasts. Afterwards they told her blatantly to make friends and to play with neighbors' kids, but she never did. Nothing had hurt her like their rejection; in the beginning, she had cried.

Later, she found a response for them. She would often crack them up with it. "They are too childish," she would often say with a seriousness that amused the adults. When they realized they couldn't send her away, they allowed her to hang around but ignored her as though she was an object that was only considered when needed. And as long as she remained quiet, she could listen to their words and jests. And because she was young and impressionable, she did copy all of what she learned from them. She imbibed their mannerisms; she took after their words. And like a stretched elastic string that had reached its breaking point, she could no longer be like kids her age.

So, when the teachers and her fellow students said that she was socially awkward, it didn't bother her. Nothing bothered her. Just as she told her grandmother's friends, her conclusion was still the same: they were all childish. Her grandmother had told her that she would outgrow it. Her parents called it a phase, and they all had watched their prediction fail and falter. She neither outgrew it nor surpassed the phase. She became cartilage that had calcified into a bone, a soft mortar that hardened. Which is why her friendship with Andre surprised her.

"You will not believe what was happening there?" Andre said as he returned to their shared workspace with a blaze of exasperation and floral perfume.

"What?" Ana responded.

"A guy was angry that the girl he asked out said no to him," he said almost as loud as the people he had gone to hush.

"Wow," Ana retorted. Not because it was unbelievable but because she somehow felt empathetic for the person who suffered the unrequited love.

"Yes," he answered her. "He was trying to cause a scene," he explained further, oblivious of how she was feeling.

"Guys and toxic masculinity," he said. Ana could detect the dark cloud that settled across his face as he said that. He once had a boyfriend who refused to leave after asking Andre to break up.

"Shh," Ana shushed him again as his voice rose.

"So, what do you think happened to Gabriella and Bernd," he segued as he settled into a seat. Ana guffawed. She thought he would forget what they were talking about before he left, but she knew that it was impossible. The Andre she knew would rather skip a meal than forget a conversation.

Ana had been thinking about that all week. The fact that she found out they abruptly stopped visiting the restaurant had made her fear the worse. In the moments that she actually thought deeply about how involved she was in the lives of these strangers, she wondered about what really happened to them.

She remembered how she had hurriedly searched the diary, flipping from page to page, fingering date after date and line after line to search for the evidence, anything. She knew from the books she had read and the movies she had watched that clues were sometimes hidden in plain sight. And she was confident that the clue that would lead her to uncover the story behind the couple's fate would be either in the diary or in the stack of documents. But when Andre asked her the questions, she was as clueless as him. All she had were possibilities.

"I really don't know," she confessed. "I think they were either kicked out or kidnapped by the communist police. Or by the Soviet sex toy suppliers," she whispered sadly. "Please hand me those books." She motioned to the pile of new books they had both unboxed earlier. No matter what she imagined had happened to them in the past, the piles of boxes reminded her that she had work to do in the present. She was glad that he was around; if he wasn't, entering the books' information into the computer would have been so daunting, even if she had help from any of the other staff. That's one thing that she loved about working with Andre. Regardless of the arduousness of the work, she realized that their closeness made the most difficult tasks easy.

"It means you haven't found anything yet?" he asked her.

"I haven't... I would have told you if I had," she replied matter-of-factly as she collected the stack of hardback volumes from him.

"You know," he began. He turned to face her, suspending his task of unboxing the new books. Ana primed her ears like an animal listening to a strange sound. Whenever Andre began a sentence with, "You know," she knew that he had something serious to say, and she wanted to know what it was this time.

"I'm all ears," she said, pulling her ears. He smiled at the act. It was a personal joke between them.

"I was reading this book... I can't seem to remember the title or author." He shut his eyes and snapped his fingers as though he was trying to summon the information from thin air.

So, what did the book say? Ana wanted to ask but allowed patience to calcify the words into thoughts. She was a little disappointed that what he mentioned was a book and not something vital that would help her. She nodded to urge him on.

"I'll let you know when I remember what the title is," he said regretfully, his face scrunched up in annoyance. She knew how much he hated to forget things, how much he loved to get his facts right at all times.

"Sure...sure," she finally spoke; she could feel the mix of annoyance and nervousness rise within her.

"I read that back then in East Berlin, people with sexual peculiarities, people who I assume would be their clients, were sometimes mean and cruelly abusive," he said in a tone that showed that he believed this was the case. He ran his tongue over his lips, and if it was another time, she would have teased him about his fascination with his lips.

So, what's the point? Ana's inquisitive mind stamped its foot angrily like a child refused its snack. He continued. Ana nodded to let him know that she was following.

"So, I think Gabriella's clients knew they were doing something wrong, so they tried to blackmail them," he added. "So, it was just normal for them to run from their blackmailers." Andre sounded like a lawyer building a case. "Or maybe the communist police caught up with them," he suggested again, another attempt of his to convince her.

You don't have to try so hard to convince me. Ana wanted to tell him, but she decided against it when she saw that he still had something to say.

"I read about several similar cases like that," he added as he saw the lack of conviction on her face.

Ana's mind spun like a gyroscope as she mulled about the possibility, the factuality of this particular theory. Her mind traveled back to science class. In high school, her science teacher taught them how scientists considered every hypothesis (every puzzle) and theory until an experiment (a test or a series of tests) was conducted to verify its authenticity. Scientists often conduct experiments to come to the truth or call a hypothesis a truth. It is after experiments that scientists call hypotheses a law or a fact. No matter how convincing her thoughts had been, no matter how realistic Andre's story had sounded to her also, she knew that it was all an assumption.

"Don't you think that this is what happened?" Andre inquired impatiently. She could see the disappointment in the droop of his eyes, in the curling of his lip.

"I think it is a possibility," she answered, acting like her teacher as said scientists often did.

She wiped her forehead with her hand. She asked herself why she was so fixated on their lives, so much so she always felt her body reacting. At that moment, she felt the beginning of a headache in her temples, and she knew that it would only get worse if she didn't stop thinking about it for a while.

"It's more than a possibility... I think that it is true," Andre said, his eyes blazing with a conviction that he wished she also had.

"They had no intention of fleeing to the west?" she said in confusion. She wasn't convinced.

If there was anything that Ana knew she had gotten from his narrative, it was the fact that she would only be convinced if she saw the book which he read the account from. But from what she observed, she realized that Andre could neither remember the book nor the author; she doubted if such a book even existed. Yet there was the fact that Andre never told lies.

"I think that we should get back to work," she suggested as she leaned back in her chair. The weight of the couple's disappearance suddenly pressed down on her. *It just feels so overwhelming,* she mused as she cracked her neck and shut her eyes. She wished she would disappear into the darkness she was plunged into when she shut her eyes.

"Just think about it," Andre insisted, still fixed on her with his why-don't-you-believe-me gaze.

Not in the mood to argue, not even in the mood to talk about the issue anymore, she nodded in acquiescence.

A loaded silence hovered between them as they returned to their tasks. Ana busied herself and remembered when she had first started working at the library, they had been warned sternly to pay attention to this aspect of the work. Once the books have been entered into the library's record system, they can be easily tracked. They were told, "You people are the gatekeepers." Those were the exact words that the trainer had said. But even if she wasn't told,

Ana often considered herself a self-motivated person and took the job seriously just the way she did everything. And since the training, she had tried to the best of her ability to do just that. To act as the perfect gatekeeper for the books. She thought about how much she loved the job, even if there were moments when it felt so boring and difficult. She just always found something to motivate her. Somedays, it is Andre, other days, it is often the most mundane thing.

At the moment, it was the scent of the new books which wafted into her nostrils. She paused for a while and savored it before flipping through the pages. Yet again, that feeling of flipping from page to page satisfied her in a way that food cannot.

"Hopeless bibliophile." Andre nudged her arm.

And it was then that the idea occurred to her. Later, she would wonder why she had not thought about it before. Wild-eyed and excited, she turned to Andre. "I'm going to do something nasty," she said.

"And what will that be?" he asked her with the enthusiasm of someone hoping to hear something salacious.

"I'm going back to the trash can where I found the diary and documents, and I will find out who owns them," she added.

7: HELP IS HERE

Ana woke to the shrill sound of chiming from her annoying phone alarm. A sound that she eventually stopped after snoozing it several times with the swipe of her hand as though she was attacking an errant fly. *Another morning,* she thought.

Ana had her mind fixed on one thing: returning to the site where she found the diary. Only she knew the possibility of doing that on that day was as slim as a knife's edge. "I hate busy days," she huffed as she swung the comforter off and rolled out of the bed, which seemed to invite her to spend more time in it.

Already, her mind had swung from that one thing to several others in that waking moment. The image of the boxes of books, the memories of her and Andre stacking, indexing, and arranging them, tugged at her mind. And then, there was the staff meeting scheduled for that day.

When will I even have the time to go back to that place? she wondered as her feet settled into the warm comfort of the shaggy rug that she had for as long as she had lived there.

Her mornings were always like this, and she also knew that getting ready for work was the hard part; once within the library walls, her reservations usually dissolved like ice in the summer sun. Ana loves her job but hates waking up and joining the hustle of daily life en route to the library.

Her eyes landed on the dog-eared diary that sat comfortably on her faded and severely chipped-on-all-sides pink bedside shelf that she had since she was little. The memories of how she had fallen in love with pink, like most girls of that age, always made her smile, considering that she no longer had any pink outfits. She remembered faintly how she had picked up the diary to read the night before, only to discover that the only thing her eyes could do was close. She wondered why she hadn't found it splayed out on the bed like some of her novels or squashed underneath her body like other unfortunate ones.

I must have placed it there before I drifted off. Just a few lines, she thought to herself. *Fifteen minutes at most,* she further convinced herself as her fingers curled around the familiar worn leather binder. She glanced at her phone to confirm if she had much time, especially with the day's events. There was time, but she also realized that she would have to sacrifice breakfast and makeup. *Anything for Gabriella,* she mused with a fanatic fervor that had gripped her since she discovered the diary. With that, she swung open the book.

The days after those men came to our house, the days after the police drifted into our home like the draft of an ominous wind, were the most sensitive days for us. The fear wore off gradually the way a stain dissipates from a cloth. But we were never the same. I, for one, wasn't. The fear may have worn off, but even stains often leave traces like invisible maps—proof of something that once was. I still couldn't go back to my shop; I couldn't see or attend to anyone. I still ensured that the doors were locked and bolted and blinds were always drawn. And even if we didn't talk about it, it hung in the air like the stench of mold in an attic, like strong perfume a long while after it had been sprayed. There were moments when I saw the cloud of fear on Bernd's face, especially at the sound of a knock on the door. But I let things be. That is one thing I have learned that I also always tell the women I attend to. Be sensitive to the moods of your spouse; that is one of the best ways to enjoy marital bliss and, of course (wonderful sex).

Bernd returned to his work. It was easy for him; his work had never been a threat. The government had nothing against gardeners or anyone who did legal work. Our other line of work was the problem. So, I was the one that had free time on my hands; I was the one that had to adjust my line of work.

A wash of excitement had flooded over us (me especially) after we had helped our first patient, that weeping woman, in the days that followed the invasion of our home. And even after she left, amidst the fear, I still wished for others to come.

Many things may have changed, but our love life has remained the same. It had remained as unchanged as the surface of an aged rock. Thinking about it now, I would say it had even gotten better. It felt as though, having realized that the worse could happen, we had both resigned to making every moment between us our best moment.

As I write these words, my body still flutters like a leaf in the path of a wind, like the surface of a rippled stream. My body still feels sore yet satisfied, my throat still feels raw and tender from the moans and groans that had escaped from my mouth, and droplets of tears still linger at the corners of my eyes—tears of joy mingled with pleasure, of course. Even my body is a stream filled with salty sweat and fresh water.

How it had begun was still a surprise to me; how we had gone from just waking up and kissing ourselves good morning to making our bed shudder in the throes of sex still puzzled me.

I discovered quite early that one of the things every person in love often gets accustomed to is the smell of their partner's morning breath. When you get familiar with the scent of your partner's morning breath, you have *stepped into a realm of intimacy. I notice that this is often a common feat for older couples but a rarity for younger ones.*

In my years of listening and attending to most individuals, I have noticed how it is little things such as this that stop wondrous things from happening. Things like a partner being unable to stand the stench of morning breath, the other finding the smell of a partner who had just returned from work irritating. While I understand that sex is better when everything smells better, I also understand that spontaneous sex is the best. And what else is unexpected, spontaneous sex except when it occurs in the presence of these factors? If I have a secret, this is one of the secrets of the wondrous sexual experiences between myself and my strong darling Bernd.

That morning, our bodies, still warm as milk and fresh and strong from a sweet night's rest, were pressed together in our daily morning ritual of kissing each other good morning when the blaze of passion erupted.

I still remember how Bernd's soft lips grazed against mine, how his strong hands cradled my face, and how his strong arms pressed against my nipples. Instead of repulsion at the scent of his morning breath, what I felt, the currents that hung in the air between us, was that of an attraction.

Usually, I would allow him to hold my head while he kissed me. On some days, my hands would be on his shoulder, against his stubble, or against fresh skin if he had shaved the day before. In these moments, my eyes would usually be shut as I savored his kiss. But I could remember that my eyes were open this morning as his clammy tongue slid into my mouth. Perhaps it was the delight that shone on his face; perhaps it was the bliss that brightened his features that ignited the spark within me. Perhaps it was the warmth of his body against mine, the feeling of safety that bloomed all over my body like fresh flowers with the way my head was cradled in his hand. Perhaps it was everything. But I had kissed back hungrily with the same intensity of the fire that was burned within my skin.

Another thing most partners fail to realize is how much selfishness can affect sex. Bernd and me practiced a form of selflessness. Rather than each of us ravaging each other's bodies to satisfy our own desires, we attended to the desires of the other. And just like every time, this paid off. Perhaps it is true what I once heard, everything is indeed better when shared—even sex. So as my hand slid over the work-chiseled contours on Bernd's body, his hands also slid beneath the silky nightgown that had encased my body.

When one's lover is only concerned with their pleasures, they will fail to realize that the body is like a maze of sensory parts, that each zone can be combined or fondled separately to make their partner enjoy sex as a heaven-on-earth experience.

As I write now, I remember as my nightgown fell off my body as though it was ash from a burning paper, how Bernd's tender yet stubby fingers had traced fire down from my collarbones to my throbbing breasts. My Bernd is a handyman, but with me, his hands are as nimble as those of a surgeon. Those were the hands that discovered that the areas in my collarbone were pleasure points. Like a well-trained dog, he had responded to my gasp of pleasure with a move that made my eyeballs spin within their sockets, and my toes curl like the shriveled skin of a fruit.

I must have screamed like a banshee when his lips took the place of his fingers and his hands cradled my breast. As I melted underneath his intense touch, I remembered pulling his body towards mine as though it was a raft in the swirling sea of desire.

One more thing that I wish all men knew is the fact that a woman's breasts should be treated the way precious gems should. Bernd knew this, and, on some days, I let him explain this to confused men that visit.

There is no way I would forget how my heart beats in my chest like the hooves of escaping war horses or those of migrating animals.

When he finally entered my temple, I already felt like sleeping again and waking up so that we could begin the precious moments once again.

On days like today, we usually showered together, not just to wash the sweat and every other bodily fluid off our bodies, but sometimes to continue from where we stopped, to spend as much time possible with each other before Bernd heads out. But today, instead of another round of sex, we chose to wash our bodies instead and talk about how spontaneous and wonderful the sex was.

Less than an hour later, Bernd headed out, leaving me to an empty house and a mind full of sweet memories.

This was the state I was in when I heard the knock. Even if the knock was gentle, it still scared the hell out of me. My eyes flew to the old grandfather clock in the corner of the room as though whatever time I would see there would also reveal who the knocker was. All I saw was 12:00. Noon. I knew that it wasn't Bernd; his knocks were confident and rhythmic; I knew it wasn't the police either; their knock on that day was sharp, and if it had any rhythm to it, it was the rhythm of urgency. This knock was soft and tentative, as though the knocker was unsure about his destination. It reminded me of my customers. Perhaps it was this realization that eased the storm that was already brewing in my stomach.

I made it to the door in a few quick strides. My eyes took in the state of the living room and my outfit as I did. Apart from a lopsided pillow, everything seemed in place. When my face pressed against the peephole, I saw the unfamiliar face of a young boy who was too old to be a teenager and too young to be an adult. "Is this Gabriella's?" he had asked tentatively in a tone that all first-time visitors often use.

"Who's asking?" I asked him as my eyes roamed from his face to the ambient environment. I had met so many people, but I was sure that I hadn't seen him before.

"Müller. Frank Müller," he had replied as though he expected me to know him. "I was told that you could help me."

I thought about asking him about the "who" and the "how," but I soon realized, both of us realized, that the longer he spent outdoors, the worse it could get for us. I reserved my question for another time, and with a mix of nervousness and excitement, I nodded.

I let him into the house after certifying that he had come alone, and even as he entered our living room, my eyes had traveled the length of the street behind him, looking, searching for a strange sight, an oddity of any kind again. I always notice it on their faces, even before they speak. That mix of despondence and expectation always chiseled in their brows, stretching their eyes taunt, pressed heavily on their shoulders, and when they finally speak, their desperation so obvious in their voices.

He sat down almost immediately as soon as I offered him a seat, partly because of exhaustion or because he imagined that taking a seat would make me attend to him immediately. And a look at his dusty feet showed me that he had walked down here. "Help me," he said as though he was in a ditch, and I was the only one to save him.

"Iced tea or water?" I asked him, pretending as though I didn't hear him. For a second, he paused, fixing me with the sort of look that people give to stubborn children or an idiot. When he noticed the look on my face, he finally acquiesced. "Water," he answered. "I'll have water."

One thing I have noticed with everyone that has visited, every client I have attended to over the years, is that the best of conversations, the clearest of communication, always occurs when people are relaxed. They never know it as much as I do, and because I know that, because I have an inkling of something that they do not, I always ensure that they are always calm before I attend to them.

I arrived with two cups of water, one for myself and another for him. I handed one to him before placing the tray on the stool beside us. I couldn't help but watch his Adam's apple move as the water traveled down his obviously parched throat. The sound it reminded me of was the sound of a fish out of water. I made a mental note to include all these details when I later told Bernd about my day. With his eyes closed as though he was doing something else other than drinking water, I had a chance to look at him slowly.

His shoes were dusty but new, his clothes neat and not overly flashy, his face had a five-o-clock shadow, and I could tell that he was handsome and young, not in an exclusive way, but in a regular way. I wondered what he wanted. Most of my clients are usually women or couples; men and boys like him rarely come. As they often assume, it is only women that have problems that men never do. A big joke.

"So why are you here, Frank?" I asked him the question that I knew he wanted so dearly to hear from me.

"Help me," he said again, as though he couldn't say any other words, as though he didn't understand a word I said.

"I will," I answered him. "Help me to help you," I added, shifting to the edge of the seat so that our knees almost touched.

Even before my question slid out of my lips, his words slipped out with the speed of semen ejaculated from a penis. "She will leave... she will leave me," he blurted in a voice that was whittled down to a whine, and before I knew it even, the whines became sobs. I watched as the sobs wracked his body like electric currents surging through a circuit. One never gets familiar with such sights, and as always, my heart clenched and unclenched within my chest as my hands found his shuddering shoulders. I felt my eyes mist.

Nothing is as touching as tears running from a man's eyes.

"She won't," I assured him, the way I had assured several men and even women that had sat across from me heaving, huffing, and hurting on the same couch. I have realized that hope is as powerful and useful as a raft, especially in times like this.

A part of me knew I was right; another part didn't believe the words I said.

"She will," he barked at me, looking at me with his blood-red eyes. "She told me that if I finished too quick again, she would." He added as the last of his tears settled on the front of his shirt.

"She won't," I assured him again, and this time, my voice was deeper, and I hoped more convincing.

He nodded, perhaps remembering that whoever had recommended me must have told him about how successful I was in whatever I did.

His answer to me was a deep exhale that shook his body like the surface of the water, which a wave had just crossed over.

I nodded to the water, and as he poured himself a cupful, I prepared the first question for him.

I am no miracle worker, nor am I a magician, so I always choose to ask questions to find out all I need about my client's condition before describing or prescribing anything to them.

Their answers become my smoke and mirrors, and their responses become my Wicca board and amulet.

"So, how long has this quick ejaculation been occurring," I asked him. In my line of work, shame is often the least considered factor, at least for me. But I could tell that he had not thought about speaking to a woman about his premature ejaculation.

"Not too long ago," he squeaked in response, his cheeks red with embarrassment. I watched him clutch the arm of the chair as though he was holding the hand of a loved one. I should look away, but I don't. I do not want him to think that his condition is something to be ashamed of. Shame and fear are twin sisters, and they are both destructive in the roles they play.

I listened as he told me what I had already suspected. By the time he was done, I could tell that he was just another case. From experience, premature ejaculation is often a result of poor dietary choices and also the most important but often the least factor—the man's psyche.

I knew even before he responded to my question about it. He loved his girlfriend, a fellow student. The way his face lit up when he spoke about her, about how they met, brought smiles several times to my face also.

He was like most young people whose diet was either funny or unstructured. His diet, if I could call such a diet, was mainly carbohydrates. I told him to work on his diet first. I told him to replace all the carbohydrates with nuts, legumes, and vegetables. I didn't expect him to jump at that, especially because he was an addicted drinker and smoker and unconcerned about his health. I told him to cut those out first. But I told him in a tone of a mother and an expert how that is perhaps the most important step to take if he wanted to stand the chance of not losing his lover. He nodded, and I could tell from the look on his face that my threat worked.

Then, I went to the next step, the part I knew he had been waiting for. I told him what I had told every man, including Bernd when he also had experienced this same condition.

I told him how to reduce his excitement. Sex is so exciting, I told him and especially if you are experiencing that with someone you love. I told him how he should feel the excitement without letting it affect his organ. His face showed me that he didn't understand me. So, I taught him a simpler method.

I taught him how to stimulate his penis before sex using one of the sample fake penises that I still had in the house. His attention was even more rapt than a sniper soldier at the battlefront as I illustrated how stimulation should continue till the point of ejaculation.

I told him how he or his girlfriend could squeeze the end of his penis before he ejaculates, especially the part where the head joins the shaft. I watched his head bob in agreement as he took it all in.

Most of my techniques are all tested and trusted, and it is with this confidence that I always tell new clients. I have seen all of them work like magic. If they hadn't worked, there was no way I would have recommended them to him. I made sure to remind him of this. For a while, I almost laughed as he nodded so quick, like a lizard of some sort. But what was most remarkable was the dark cloud that lifted from his brow.

I told him and showed him how to keep squeezing the area for as long as possible (I told him to count up to ten seconds) until the urge to ejaculate passed. When the door finally shut, he wasn't the only one with a smile on his face. Once again, I was reminded why I didn't mind

risking my and, indeed, our lives. I loved what I did, and most importantly, I loved making people happy.

•••••••

All through the ride to the office, Ana couldn't take her mind off what she read. The words, the tale, the experience, and the lessons all swirled in her mind like dust in the wind. A while back, she had thought about jotting down the crucial points, but she had waved away the thought as soon as they came. Anything other than reading, imbibing, and ingesting all she read from the diary would only serve as a distraction; that was her conclusion. So, she had settled for reading alone.

Sitting on her bed that morning, her breath still sour and clammy from the night before, her bedsheets still tangled and sweat-stained, her room as messy as it always was. She had hoped to only spend a few minutes and to read a few pages which described what she did most mornings. But as the cab slowed down, she discovered that few had become much, and much had resulted in time spent. As she predicted, she had had to skip breakfast and experience Flora's protest. She smiled as she recalled Flora's words. "You will get so thin that no one will want to marry you." *Marry, marry, marry, is that the only thing you guys want from me?* she had almost screamed at her, but she hadn't. The memories of their past row were still fresh in her mind. So, she told her the part truth, I woke up a little bit late, so

I would be late if I waited to eat. She hated hearing the word "marry" and wished Flora knew that much about her. But it is something that she had learned about adults, Flora included; they all seemed to always dismiss her thoughts (sometimes with a casual wave of the hand).

Thinking about that morning, she realized she had spent almost thirty minutes more than she should have spent reading through Gabriella's tale of her encounter with the student. She recalled how she had blushed when the diary's content made her imagine what sex would be like with Theo.

She had thought about it several times. And several questions popped up in her mind, questions such as...

Will Theo be the kind of partner that could last longer?

Was he the kind that also suffers from quick ejaculation?

Can she know all this by merely looking at him?

She didn't know any of the answers to the questions, yet the thought of how to get the answers even made her blush the more.

I shouldn't be thinking of that, she tried to control herself.

She bolted from the cab as soon as she had settled with the driver and rushed into the lobby that led to the library.

She hated being late and was already prepared for whatever Mr. Novak would do to her. She always preferred his rants to his cold stares. She knew that if she had a choice not to choose between either, she would have chosen that option, but there wasn't.

As she slid into the library, she was relieved when she discovered he wasn't there. She didn't even mind that he would see her on the monitor in his office.

He's so creepy, she thought to herself as she slid into her seat, separated by the pile of books that seemed like a wall of some sort between her and Andre.

"Don't tell me you went there this morning," Andre said as he peeked behind the pile as soon as she sat down.

"Of course, no," Ana replied with genuine horror. "Who digs into people's trashcan so early in the morning," she spat out with a face crinkled like a squeezed piece of paper.

"Well, someone desperate for answers like you," he said as he extended his hands for a good morning handshake.

Ana took his hands and was happy that he was so busy that he didn't insist on his usual hug and a peck on each cheek. She knew he would still ask for it when they were less busy.

"You are right about one thing, yet you are wrong about another," she whispered as she picked up the first book in the pile, a revised version of the *Handmaid's Tale*.

"Tell me, Ana," Andre said without looking her way. Whatever hope she had nursed for a quiet morning was slowly flowing down the drain.

"I want to know everything about Gabriella and her partner and everyone connected to them." With that reference, she meant the gay couple whose disappearance still bothered her as though they were her friends or relatives. That is how much she had become connected to the story, how much she took the diary seriously.

"But I'm not so desperate to go into the rubbish dump to go find the other documents as you assumed," she replied as she entered a book's serial number into the computer.

"Oh please," Andre tutted. "This is something I know you're desperate about," he teased her.

"I don't blame you, Andre... I blame myself for telling you about the diary," she added as she picked her second book, a hard copy version of George Orwell's classic *Animal Farm*.

"You have no choice, Ana.... I'm your only best friend," Andre whispered as though he had suddenly realized how loud his voice was. "And whenever you decide to go, just make sure you do not go without me," he added. With a few more banters exchanged between them, they soon settled into a work-inspired silence.

Almost an hour later, Ana blurted out the thoughts spinning through her mind all morning. "You never even asked why I was late this morning?" she said to the busy Andre.

"I must have forgotten," he answered, his intense blue eyes searching Ana's face.

"You had a fight with Flora, or you visited Theo," Andre teased.

"That's not a question." Ana rolled her eyes at him and wished that she hadn't brought up the matter. But she knew that it was impossible. Having a secret she couldn't share with him was like keeping water in a basket. Andre could be the most amazing friend, but she also knew how annoying he could be. And he seemed to be on his worst behavior at that moment.

"Come on darling... why are you so sensitive this morning?" He blew her a mock kiss accompanied by a wink.

"Because you are so annoying," she responded as the ghost of a smirk appeared on her face.

"Okay, why were you late?" he asked. Ana exhaled, leaned into her chair, lifted her eyes to see if Mr. Novak or any of the supervisors were anywhere close, and she began her tale.

"Are you sure I won't steal this book from you?" Andre asked teasingly as soon as Ana was done.

"You wish," she replied to him. "I have a question," she whispered as soon as their muffled laughter had subsided.

Andre nodded at her.

"How can I know if Theo has the same problem?" she asked the question that had prompted her to tell him the story.

Andre stifled the laughter that attempted to threaten to spill out of him.

"You will know when you finally get to have sex with him," he answered.

8: THE DISCOVERY

"This feels like the most interesting part of a mystery or thriller movie," Andre yelped excitedly with the enthusiasm of a child visiting Disneyland for the first time as they gathered their things.

"You know that part when ominous music plays and one's heart leaps to their throat," he continued. Ana knew that he would have demonstrated further by miming the soundtrack if she hadn't looked at him the way that she did.

Who even uses ominous in a sentence? she wondered. Only Andre, of course, she concluded.

His eyes were brighter than the lights in the room, even almost more luminous than the sun. His voice rose, echoing loudly in the almost empty room. She was now familiar with his range of emotions, extremely happy as a lark when happy and sad as a dreary dark night when sad. And, as always, she was pleased that he was the former, not the latter.

The thrill from finally closing and returning home was very high, especially with how long and tiring their day had been. Neither of them loved the long and vapid meeting or the fact that more boxes of new books were wheeled in as they filed out of the meeting room.

More work this week, Ana thought to herself, her face adopting an I-am-so-pissed mask.

"Does it ever end?" These were the exact words Andre said as they watched the boxes being unloaded by uniformed muscular men who seemed as tired as them. If Andre had looked at her face, he would have known that she was as pissed as he was. But he hadn't; his attention had drifted to his phone, which had just beeped.

Does it really? Ana thought quietly to herself as they both hurried back to their desk. She was too tired to answer him. All she wanted was to get out of the library complex and make it to the trashcan. All she desired was to make it to that house with that trashcan where she had picked up the diary, the trashcan that had changed her life. Around them, the library was already a shadow of itself—empty desks, vacated seats, just a trickle of individuals in a place that before was occupied by many. The vast space would have been deathly quiet the way Ana loved it if not for the hum of the old air-conditioning units and the shuffle of exiting feet. Ana could see the color of the sky from the window; the sun had dropped its austere stare leaving the sky a faded orange color.

She knew that the sky would soon turn the grey of marble. Orange meant promising; grey meant the color she dreaded yet hoped for—night. The night will provide the perfect cover of darkness, but it will also be a disadvantage. If they were caught rifling through a stranger's trashcan so late, anything could happen. For a while, she allowed her eyes to linger on the cloud of dust particles caught in the sun's glare. If and when it finally settled on the surfaces, they would be evidence of one of the ways she could confirm if the cleaners did any work. There used to be a time when they had a cleaner who was always lying about cleaning. She returned her gaze to the room. The last of the people still around were also doing exactly what they were doing, clearing their desks, stuffing their books underarms, or shuffling their feet as they made a beeline for the door. Moments earlier, they had done one of the closing rituals—moving from aisle to aisle to check and confirm if everything was in place. They had seen what they expected, empty tables, a few belongings like pens and notepads left behind, and definitely trash left behind for the cleaners who often worked late at night and early the following day.

It really does, Ana thought as she considered Andre's words.

"Or a scene from a mystery book," Ana added as she tucked her water bottle into its compartment in her bag. She had been able to skip breakfast that morning, but Flora had ensured she went with her bottle. She smiled wistfully as the memories floated to her mind's surface.

"Water is life; you mustn't leave the house without this, at least." Flora pushed the bottle into Ana's hands. Even without looking at her, Ana knew how furrowed her brows would be, how squinted her eyes would be as though she was daring her to defy her order even if both of them knew that it was no order. So, she had taken it, and just when she thought it was over, Flora had added. "Ensure you drink it." Ana had drunk it before she had lunch during lunch, and afterward. Not because she wanted to be the archetypical obedient granddaughter but because it was summer and everywhere was dry.

"Right," he answered. His excitement tripling as she acquiesced. "And we are the two protagonists, the hero, and her sidekick," he added with the same excitement that made Ana roll her eyes at him again.

"This is real life, Andre," she told him.

"I know, which is why I have been meaning to ask," he said as he turned to her, his mood changing as he did.

"Ask what exactly?" she turned, paying attention to him.

"What if the trash can is empty when we get there?" Andre asked suddenly as his eyes made a final sweep of the library.

Ana could brag about being passionate as a librarian, and she did almost all the time, but Andre was the one who took his work seriously with military precision.

"Well, we will go to the house and ask whoever we may find there if they know anything," Ana replied in a matter-of-fact tone as she slipped her bag over her shoulder. She ignored the fact that her voice was as sharp as the edge of a fresh blade. *Andre would understand*, she told herself; her intention wasn't to sound that way. If Andre noticed the sharpness of her tone, he said nothing. So, she ignored it and let her mind roam. Throughout the day, during the meeting and as she munched her meal midway through work, she had allowed her mind free rein of all thoughts possible. In those moments, she had thought about everything, including Andre's question.

"Woah," Andre answered, his attention returning to her. She was glad that she had told him, and he was joining her. She might have had all the answers to her questions, but she was still nervous and glad that he was right there with her.

"What?" she asked, stopping midway, her hand dropping to his shoulder.

"Your determination, your desperation about this matter is what always surprises me," he said in the tone of a person that had been meaning to tell her those exact words for a long time.

Ana let her hand slide from his shoulder and return to her bag. She had been hoping that he would say something else, something new, different, something that would be beneficial for the quest that they were about to undertake.

Ana allowed a chuckle to escape from her lips. It all felt like a déjà vu, the sight of them walking away from their desk piled high with books, a reminder of the busy future that awaited them. Her clothes felt the same, cotton ankle-length pants paired with a matching chiffon top. Andre's clothes were also the same, a light pastel-colored sweatshirt tucked into well-fitted chinos pants that ended on top of the horse bit loafers he wore.

Before she met him, she had imagined herself the impeccable dresser, the kind of person who looked the same way in the evening as they had in the morning, but she discovered that he was something else. Andre was the type to wear a pearly white shirt no matter how long the day was. He was the kind to still have the pleat on his pants unruffled on the same day. And they would usually always both laugh about it, especially when she teased him about it. "Teflon don," she would always call him. The one on whom dirt and crease don't stick. But she wasn't in the mood for such banter, especially not at that moment.

"I know," Ana replied as they headed past the sliding door of the library into the warmth of the evening weather.

The motion-sensitive lights that usually came on, especially after hours, went off behind them. The arriving cleaners waved at them, and they both nodded back. The temperature difference caused their skin to bristle, but neither of them paid attention to it. The quiet that had constituted a major part of their day gave way to the noise of a busy city at night.

"Whatever you are accusing me of and about... I am very much guilty of it," Ana replied in a voice that was utterly free of animosity. She had thought about it long and hard almost every day, and she had come to the same conclusion. There was absolutely nothing in her past or present that she had invested so much of her time or divested so much of her attention as she had done with uncovering all the secrets surrounding Gabriella. *It's personal to me, this pursuit of truth,* Ana thought.

"I'm glad that you finally agreed; now let's go get the remaining parts of that diary," Andre said, rubbing his hands in excitement. He did that thing that made both of them burst into a peal of uproarious laughter right there by the roadside—he mimed an ominous movie soundtrack.

•••••••••

When they arrived where Ana found the diary, the sky was the color of a shadow—starless and gloomy. Unlike the pitch darkness of the first night, Ana noticed a sliver of visibility, reflections from the lit windows of the houses looked like the yellow eyes of a reptile, and then there was also a subdued golden sheen from the streetlights that were working. Ana looked around, reacting to the nervousness that had gripped her the last time she was there. Apart from the gaunt stooped figure of the burnt-out street lights looming in irregular places, everything seemed right.

The street beneath her was smooth as she could remember it, free from potholes and unusual bumps, yet the grit crunched almost too loudly beneath their feet as they made their way toward the house.

Aside from that, the street was empty, quiet, and almost deserted like it was on the night she had stumbled upon the marble statue, the night she had stumbled into the lives of Gabriella and Bernd. The summer season had its advantages, and in moments like this, Ana realized why she hated its disadvantages more—the prickly heat that made her clothes stick to her body uncomfortably, the balminess of the air that made one want to run from the street and find the closest air-conditioning unit. She knew she would have worn something lighter, perhaps shorter if she wasn't coming from work. She would have worn anything that made her feel as comfortable as possible.

Global warming, she mulled as she recalled the online article she had read a few days ago about the earth becoming hotter and other quasi-apocalyptic predictions, like some cities sinking slowly and the Sahara Desert expanding. "Que sera, sera," she had whispered that day with the passivity of a stoic after reading. Back in the present, she ignored the discomfort in her body and focused on the task at hand. Like a sidekick in a real movie, she couldn't help but wonder why Andre had suddenly fallen silent, but she let it be. What she needed was his company, his keen sense of sight, and his hands.

Like she had expected, the disorderly pile stared them in the face as though begging to be rifled through, daring her to sift through it again. "Look at me, touch me," the pile seemed to say.

It's looking bigger, she observed as she inched towards it, Andre following closely behind her like a detective approaching a crime scene.

She could see the rectangular lights in the windows of the neighboring houses around them. When she peered keenly, she could see the activity within—shadowy figures moving around their homes, interacting with each other, totally shut out from the world that they had toiled in all day (or so they thought). She could see them, only she wasn't interested in them. Her quest was the diary, not the secret lives of the street's inhabitants.

"Do you know exactly what we are looking for?" Andre enquired, breaking his seemingly sworn oath of silence for the first time.

They were at the edge of the pile; the house the debris was situated in front of was lit by a single bulb; its golden rays reflected through the pane of grimy glass. She looked intently at the glass, but apart from the light's reflection, there was nothing else that she could see. Nothing could tell her if the house was inhabited or not.

"Like I said before, I am looking for all the lost parts of the diary," Ana replied. She ignored the slight irritation that crawled within her belly as she remembered that she had told Andre several times about their mission here.

"Okay," he replied as his eyes scanned the neighborhood again like a vigilant thief scared of being caught. She could hear his breath catch, and she wanted to laugh at his earlier boast. "I will be the best sidekick ever," he had said when they were barely five minutes away. "Don't you think we should knock first and find out who lives here and why their trash is being emptied out here," he asked in a voice that showed how much caution he was exercising. In his words, she could hear the words unsaid.

We could be arrested for trespassing, we could be shot at, and someone could be watching us.

For the umpteenth time, Ana wondered why she had brought him along. Yet again, she wondered if she would have come with anyone else. Apart from him, she had no other friends. Her other friends were old and probably snoring in their beds, reading bedtime stories to their grandkids, or like Flora, glancing at the clock awaiting the arrival of their grandkids. *That's what I get for rolling with geriatrics.* Ana teased herself in a moment of self-introspection.

The other people that knew about the diary were Flora and Theo. The thought of bringing this up with her grandmother or asking Theo to come with her to this nighttime rendezvous was both funny and inconvenient. Flora would poo-poo the idea with the wave of her hand, and Theo might agree, but she wasn't sure she wanted to share this experience with him. She would have to manage Andre, she told herself. After all, someone once said that when the desirable isn't available, the available become desirable. At no time had that aphorism seemed more apt than at this present moment.

"I thought about that." Ana bent her knee so she could begin riffling through the pile of papers she had been standing in front of like a sentry guarding a precious stone. She glanced at Andre, whose eyes were still sweeping across the street. "But I thought I should search first, and if we don't find what we are looking for, we would then do that," she replied. She couldn't help but notice how she sounded like Flora—pedantic and objective. She hoped that her explanation was reasonable enough for him.

"Sounds reasonable," he said, stealing the words from her thoughts. They both chuckled knowingly. To others, "reasonable" might seem like a general word, but to them, it was more. It was an inside joke whose origin always brought the same reaction each time it occurred.

"So, will you join me or continue questioning me, sidekick?" she teased him as she swung her gaze down from his face to the pile of paper in her hands.

"Aye, aye, Captain," he responded and slid to the ground beside her. The scent of his perfume mingled with the nose-tickling smell of dust, mortar, or whatever formed the powdery particles that hung in the air around them. He grabbed a sheaf of paper in front of him, and with the aid of his phone's light turned to the lowest, he began his investigation.

Sidekick indeed, Ana wondered wistfully.

The coat of dust or powder that hung like a cloud over them and a film atop the pile stuck to her clammy palms as she peered at the papers. The light streaming from Andre's phone was low, but it was bright enough for her to see. Although no one and nothing had stirred since they got to the street, Ana knew enough not to include another source of light as much as she wanted to. One more light was enough to get anyone's attention. If there was any attention that she was looking for, it was only the attention of whoever inhabited this house. Not the attention of the neighbors and certainly not the police. So, in the spirit of improvising, she instead chose to squint her eyes and peer at the papers like some of Flora's friends would.

Where are they ... where are they? Ana wondered as she flipped from page to page, her eyes scanning the entire document length, her fingers flipping from one leaf to the other with the rapidity of a counting machine. Her hope rose with every glance, yet as she read through the document, bank statements, lease papers, detached pieces of a notebook, tattered leaves of novels—everything except a portion of the diary.

"Have you found anything?" she turned to Andre, who had been bent over digging through a pile of discarded toilet fittings. Her ears were trained for his response, her eyes fixed on his hands like the glare of a headlight. Even if she couldn't see any papers in his hands, she knew she had seen some earlier when she had looked at him.

"Nothing except manuals and some brown papers with faded words," he responded despondently. His brows furrowed and coated with dust. His response confirmed her doubt and established her fears—there was nothing left in this pile of dirt and debris.

"Let's check one more time," Ana responded, swiping the back of her hands against her face before muffling a sneeze in the crook of her elbow. Her body was tired, her knees cramped, and she felt the beginnings of an ache in her head and pressure in her nose from the accumulated dust. But as the saying goes, her spirit had no trace of weakness. It felt as though she could continue; she would continue for hours.

"If you say so," Andre replied.

"You check there," she motioned to the edge of the sea of debris. "I'll check there," she pointed to the space adjacent to where she had directed him.

He moved immediately, more out of frustration than in accordance with her instruction. His phone's light flipped in his hands and plunged them into momentary darkness. The street was as quiet as it was when they arrived. A blanket of darkness was gradually settling over the area, thanks to the lights going off in most houses. Ana didn't bother checking the time to confirm how long they had been riffling and digging rather unsuccessfully. An itch-like bother began creeping to the surface of her mind—*if there were any inhabitants of the house, wouldn't it be too late to make any enquiries*, she wondered.

They split as they headed to both ends of the overfilled trashcan and the accompanying pile that had formed beside it like a molehill of some sort.

The sounds of their hands digging made her imagine giant rats burrowing into the pile of dirt. She dug continuously, scooping, looking, and glancing toward

Andre like an egret looking for a chunk of flesh from its mother.

Each look was rewarded with disappointment after disappointment, and just as she had planned but hoped that it wouldn't get to, she knew she was left with no other option.

But if there is no one here? What if they get mad at us for knocking at this time? The thoughts scurried through her mind with the same intensity with which her hands swept through the debris. So far, the only thing that they had discovered was dust and grime, with much of it going up their noses and under their fingernails. Even before she looked at Andre, she could tell she would be the only one left alone searching for the unattainable if she did anything other than stating the obvious. Andre's decision was already lined on his wrinkle-free face. Yet the thought of knocking on a stranger's door at that time of the night worried her.

"You can never know the real situation until you try it," Flora's voice countered her indecision. And because she had followed that short but always effectual counsel all the time, she had often succeeded; she ignored the fear and did exactly what she feared.

"Let's do it," she said suddenly. The sound of the objects dropping from her hand ricocheted with a loud clang that traveled through the empty streets.

"I would have mentioned it if you hadn't," Andre huffed as he wiped his hands against his brown corduroy pants. His face was the mask of relief. The beads of sweat glistened like bright jewels in the dark.

"It is about time," she answered as she brushed the dust from her hands. "I only hope that someone is home," she added in a voice that revealed her nervousness.

"I think someone is home," Andre replied as he took his place beside her. Ana looked at him with the look of someone who expected to be pranked.

"You saw someone?" she asked, alarmed at his words, her eyes traveling along his face, searching for a sign that showed that he was joking.

"I heard voices," Andre responded. And as though to confirm that he wasn't joking, he added. "We had better knock before they meet us here." With no words to say, Ana did what she realized she should have done since they had arrived—she walked towards the door.

Their footsteps tracked along the stairs leading to the house. Ana noticed it because she glanced behind them, still expecting to see something in a pile.

"You are a stubborn optimist," Mr. Novak once said to her someday after a particularly heated brainstorming session. She believed that the library should adopt some of the emerging trends practiced in other countries to boost attendance and make the library raise its own funds.

She didn't think about it then, never had thought about it, but she knew she was the kind that never said no or backed down, especially when she was right about something or someone. There had been times when her intuition had been wrong, and like those times, she knew that she was wrong because all she saw was broken plastic, cracked tiles, and a waste bin filled to its brim with everything other than the missing leaves of the diary.

Andre was the one who knocked when they got there. She would have said something about it, a tease, a caution, something. After all, she was the one who had brought him there, but she was too tired, tense, and nervous to say anything other than to remain a spectator in a movie she had produced.

At first, all she heard was the echo of knuckles against an ancient oak door. Andre maintained his gaze.

Perhaps they are not around... perhaps we wouldn't have to have this awkward conversation, she mulled as the sounds of the knock echoed again. She tried to distract her thoughts by staring at the chipped paint falling from every part of the door. This was an old house. It was evident everywhere she looked; in the exposed bricks on the lintel, in the cracks at the corner of the glass door.

She was beginning to doubt Andre's words, wondering if tiredness had convinced him about the sights and sounds he claimed to see and hear. Then she heard them too.

If she wasn't standing right in front of the door, she would have assumed that it was something else, a breeze moving through the debris, a rat making its way to the trash can. Even if she knew that the street was too neat for rats. But she heard it, the padding of approaching footsteps, the sound of someone's voice.

Her body tensed like the tightened strings of a violin; nervousness turned her belly into a tight ball. Like melting ice cream, sweat poured down her back. *Is this even a good idea?* she asked herself for the gazillionth time.

On Andre's face was the unmistakable yet expected I-told-you-so look, and she nodded at his unsaid words.

She realized there was a peephole when a face pressed against it. For a second, she wanted to state their names and their reasons for being there without being asked, but she waited, and like objects under observation, they waited for the figure behind the door to look at them.

Instead of a voice asking them who they were, just as Ana was expecting, they were bathed in a ray of bright light. They both shrunk back, Ana more than Andre, as though the light was liquid, as though the liquid had been splashed on them.

And before they could do anything, the door swung open, revealing a mountain of a man. The three of them were caught in a staring battle at that moment. No one moved, nor did anyone speak. The air around them bristled with uncertainty. The mountain of a man covered in dust and plaster and shrouded in a paint-stained work outfit. He looked at them the way one would look at kids caught throwing eggs on that door. Ana couldn't tell if he was what she was expecting, but she hadn't thought about who the inhabitants would be.

If she ever had hoped to make a good first impression and have Mr. Hulk take them seriously, Ana knew it was then or probably never. So, she cleared her throat and asked him if he knew Gabriella and Bernd.

From how he looked at her and then at Andre, she knew he didn't. Ana felt her heart and hopes plummet.

"I don't know those people," he answered with an uninterested shrug as though Ana had asked an adult about a cartoon character. "We are merely workers," he added. The words clanged like a bell in Ana's ears. Three other men dressed in similar attire appeared from the house's innards.

Ana had thought he was the only one in the house; she had even begun to wonder if he was the lone homeowner redecorating so late in the night.

"Can we come in?" Andre asked, reminding Ana that she wasn't alone and that they would be better indoors than outdoors.

"Come in," they all chorused like overeager kids meeting their new neighbors for the first time. Ana wondered if they were excited about seeing her or Andre. She only had to glance at Andre to see him smile too profoundly at a worker with the thickest eyebrows. Inside the house were a kaleidoscope of scrapped plaster and peeling wallpapers that fell over ladders like wilted leaves of trees. Ana and Andre stepped gingerly to avoid coating themselves in paint.

"We were working late because some of us wouldn't be around tomorrow," Hulk said. The talk of Gabriella and Bernd was forgotten entirely, like the empty bottles of beer and boxes of takeout littering the floor.

Ana nodded and wondered how she would mention the reason for her visit without divulging all the details.

"If you are interested in the house, I can show you around," Mr. Hulk, who introduced himself as Hector, said. Ana would have refused if Andre hadn't said yes and stepped ahead. She made a mental note to tease him about that. *Once you see a man, you begin to act like a fish out of water*. That's what she planned to tell him. But at the moment, she followed as though she was interested. Hector in front, Andre beside him, and her behind.

He showed them the parts of the house with the practiced ease of someone who did that daily. Ana was sure she would have ignored the tour entirely if not for Andre. Her eyes and feet may have followed him, but her mind was someplace else, and it soon affected how she looked and what she looked at.

Could it be that Gabriella and Bernd lived here? If so, was it within these peeling walls and beneath this vaulted roof that they made love? If not, how did their possessions make it to the trash can? Ana wondered.

These were the questions that she had come here to find answers to. The other workers soon lost interest in them, and the sound of running water and uproarious laughter made her realize that they were either showering or washing off the accumulated grime from their bodies.

As soon as they got back to the living room, Ana blurted out, "Hector, we came here looking for a couple who may have lived here… maybe you know them?"

"Like I said before," he replied with a tone that suggested that he wasn't the kind of person who loved repeating himself. "We were hired by the realtor to clean out the house, but since you are interested in this," his paint-speckled hands hovered in the air as though he wanted to conjure Gabriella's and Bernd's names from the air. "I can give you his number," he said as he dug his giant paws into the pockets of his overalls. With the way his shoulder was turned to them, she was sure it was the end of their conversation. Ana's stomach rumbled, but it had nothing to do with hunger and everything to do with expectation.

Ana would remember that moment forever. Not the heat that made her so uncomfortable that she had imagined taking off all her clothes, not the sinking feeling that accompanied the failure at not finding the missing pages of the diary and not the tiredness and filth on their bodies. Later, Ana and Andre hugged goodbye under a sky that was darker than when they had first set out. The realtor's number saved on her phone was enough consolation for her. It was both her cold shower and clean clothes.

The next day after work, less tired and extremely curious, Ana and Andre sat across from the realtor, who glared at them, his face a perfect mask of surprise.

"We just want to know who owns the house." Ana had replied the second time after he had asked if they were interested in buying the house. Her voice was sharp and determined, as though she was daring the squinty-eyed man to turn them down. Ana could tell that he wasn't used to having visitors like them, and neither was he familiar with having requests like theirs. But she was determined not to be flustered. If he had any answers, her stubborn optimism would pull them from him, whatever the cost.

Minutes later, two other realtors, who had been engaged in another office, sauntered over to where Andre and Ana sat with the realtor.

"We are kids of the original owners, all three of us. This is our real estate company," the woman with wispy blonde hair, and an ill-fitting suit said to Ana. "Why are you looking for our parents?" she asked in a voice that was as cold as the question.

She could see Andre adjust uncontrollably in his seat. And she could only wonder what his thoughts were.

Kids? The word felt like a slap across her face. In Ana's mind, she thought, *No way... this can't be true.* Her lips were even curled. But the piercing gazes in her direction made her change her mind.

Ana couldn't tell which was the truth or which was a blatant lie. Young as she was, she already knew how dissimilar truth and lies could be. So, she bit down on her tongue and allowed her mind to roam. The room bristled with a nervous mix of suspicion, confusion, and fear. Yet Ana could feel something else—something that made her feel at ease. She recalled the parts of the diary she had read; the couple had emphatically stated that they were not interested in having kids.

Was it possible that they later had kids after their disappearance? she thought to herself. As though seeking proof, she looked from face to face trying to calculate the ages of the people around her and trying to place the resemblance.

Confused and possibly moments away from being tossed out or reported to the cops, she slipped her hands into her bag and produced a picture of the couple. Sliding the formerly glossy, slightly faded picture towards the siblings, she asked in a voice shaking with nervousness, "Do you know them?"

9: THE REVEAL

Ana had never looked keenly at anything or anyone the way she looked at the faces of the trio. If expectation had a human form, it would look like her, it would breathe like her, and its heart would pound like hers.

At the moment, between watching them look at the picture she slid between them and waiting for their responses or reactions, she felt her body grow taunt with nervousness.

For Ana, anything would have been perfect at that moment, anything apart from the beat of silence that enveloped the brightly-lit room. Later she would remember what she noticed at that moment. She would remember their faces. She would remember the moles, the birthmarks, the freckles, the faint scars, the jutting cheekbones, and rough stubble. She could tell whose nose had been broken before or the face with blemishes partially masked by makeup. It's incredible how many details the eyes can capture upon such close observation, especially in moments like that.

Yet none of what she saw was what she wanted even though those few seconds seemed so loaded, so stretched as though it was eternity, a time with no end. But she couldn't look away even if their responses seemed delayed.

She wondered what children took so long to recognize their parents, as the few seconds seemed to stretch into minutes.

If anyone had asked her what she imagined their reaction would be, she knew that it wouldn't have been what she was seeing. She ignored the annoying crawl of sweat streaming down her body or her leg shaking beside the table.

"You know that you can never get away with telling lies... you are so terrible at lying," Flora had told her once on the day that Ana had lied to her many years ago. She could remember how she had shaken so hard and averted her gaze as though her grandmother's eyes were blazing flames, even if they were as gentle as they always were. That was the last time she told a lie to Flora. And even if she wasn't lying at present, Ana couldn't help but recall that moment with Flora, thanks to her quivering feet. And she knew it was all thanks to the strange reaction from the three siblings.

She had expected eyeballs popping out of their sockets and gasps of shock escaping from parted lips. She had expected them to inquire why she had taken an interest in their parents' pictures. She had expected something, anything except what happened next.

After what seemed like an eternity, the woman in the ill-fitting suit with the sprinkling of freckles on her face spoke first.

"We know them," she answered coolly as she flicked a stray hair from her face and relaxed as though she was leaning into a chair, only there was no chair as she had been perched at the table's edge. Ana saw the other two nod their agreement. She heard Andre exhale loudly, and for a brief moment, she looked at him. In her preoccupation, she had forgotten about him. He was right; she was not only desperate, but she was also definitely wrapped up in this thing like prey in the grip of a boa constrictor.

She and Andre exchanged a brief smile which they both knew meant everything was going well.

"You know them?" Ana turned to the woman as though she hadn't heard the initial words. It was something she hated being done to her; she hated being asked a rhetorical question, but at that moment, that was the only thing she could say to shatter the silence that had settled in the room.

Her chair squeaked uncomfortably as she shifted in it. Her knees pressed against the side of the table. In her head, her thoughts settled like particles falling to the bottom of a cloudy liquid.

"Our parents, who owned the house, were also real estate agents. When they passed, I was already a realtor, so they left the business to me. Eventually, my brothers Eric and Uwe became realtors as well, and now we run the family business together."

The declaration simply meant that the diary was right; Gabriella and Bernd had no children. She felt relief seeping into the tight space that had formed in her chest.

No wonder I hadn't seen any resemblance, Ana thought.

"We do," the siblings answered in unison, confirming yet again what Ana had just discovered. Gabriella and Bernd were no parents of the trio, but who were these kids to them? That was the question that Ana wanted an answer to more than anything at that moment. She would have even chosen it over oxygen if she had been presented with the choice.

The room was as bright as it had been when they had walked in, but from the window at the far end of the room, Ana could see the sunless sky already turning a mix of blue and grey. She returned her attention to the table where a wistful smile was on the faces of three siblings staring at the picture.

She was about to ask for clarity from them, an explanation about the relationship between them and

Gabriella and Bernd, when the woman picked up the picture and brought it close to her face as though she was looking for a missing detail.

"They were the nicest people we have ever met, right, Eric?" she asked her brother. Ana let her words die on her tongue; perhaps they would reveal the relationship before she asked. The moment seemed too solemn to interrupt with the questions that rumbled in her belly like the engine of a locomotive.

"To say that they were nice was an understatement," he answered in a serious tone, the sort of tone one would use to refer to a stranger that something horrible had happened to. On his face, Ana could see the truth; a nostalgic warmth had taken the place of his poker face.

He leaned forward toward his sister and held the picture at the edge so that they both held it. Ana looked from his face, with its broken nose and the mole on the upper lip, to the other brother, who was the real estate agent they initially talked to. She wondered why he wasn't as keen as the others. She noticed that he was the youngest of the trio, and she concluded that perhaps he was too young to know the couple. She saw a new copy of Mario Puzo's *The Godfather* on the table with his finger serving as a bookmark. Of them all, she wouldn't have thought him the reader. His other siblings were dressed in corporate outfits, but he was casually dressed in a T-shirt tucked into his jeans atop a pair of construction worker boots. *He looks more like a gamer*, she thought to herself.

She was wrong and corrected herself. He *would* be the one to read a novel of the three of them. As a librarian, she should have known that. After all, most of the novel lenders were young people, people about his age or even younger. She looked away from his stubbled chin, which to her was due for shaving, and returned her attention to his siblings, who were peering into the picture with a smile that seemed to confirm their words. Gabriella and Bernd must have shared many memories with them or vice versa. Smiles could be deceptive, but she could read theirs—they were the nostalgic smiles of those who had shared happy memories.

"Uwe, don't you remember them" the woman nudged her brother a little too hard. But he barely looked up or matched their enthusiasm.

Oh, the millennials. Ana found her judgmental mind saying what it always said whenever she noticed a puerile habit done by a person. Had she not stopped judging herself, she would have queried the thought if she also wasn't a millennial. But she was way past that. She had come to accept that she was precocious and accepted it the way one accepts fate.

Ana noticed that his attention was still more on the phone than with them. Ana couldn't help but imagine what Flora would have said about him. Her words often floated to her mind every time she sees someone too caught up with their phones.

"Phones will be the end of this generation," Flora would often say with the certainty of a doomsday prophet that has never been wrong with their prophecies. And with the sort of books Ana had read, and the news about people losing their lives while using their phones at the wrong places and wrong times, Ana found out that she was almost a believer—her grandmother's proselyte. Phones may not end the generation, but she knew many who feared that technology would do more harm than good. But that was the least of Ana's worries. The suspense about their relationship with the couple was most prominent on her mind.

Ana hated the suspense, so she finally spoke. She looked at the woman, Ana's eyes meeting hers, only it was not in her typical challenging look. The look that Andre once called dare-me-if-you-can.

"The workers at the house told us that if we needed any more information, we could get it here" Ana finished. There was something almost retarded about the way she had broken her words into bits. But fluency was the least of her problems. Provided that she had expressed all that she wanted to say, she was satisfied with her effort.

The man whose name she now knew as Eric looked at her this time, he was no longer holding the picture, and instead, his hands were placed flat on the table in front of him like someone about to do pushups. She watched him lean back in his chair, and the foamy backrest creaked as though complaining about his weight. Ana couldn't help but wonder what had happened to his crooked nose, *Street fight or professional fight?* Something about him just made her believe that he was a fighter of some sort despite his suit.

"Unexpectedly, they were right. We don't think anyone can tell you more about Bernd and Gabriella than us." Ana had never felt this excited. The missing diary pages were vivid in her mind, and finding out what could possibly have happened to the couple seemed so attainable, as though she could reach out and grab it. And she couldn't wait to hear about them.

"They literally raised us." The woman took over as though she didn't want the man to continue. Ana recalled the image of Gabriella that she had in her head taking care of the younger version of the siblings. She just couldn't accept that possibility. She hadn't read anywhere in the diary a reference to neighbors' kids or anything of the sort.

"They rented our parents' house," the woman added. Ana nodded more to indicate that the woman should continue talking than out of understanding.

"Of course, we didn't live with them," the woman added as though her response was an afterthought. She adjusted a straying tress again and her position on the table. "But they showed us so much love whenever we visited the house," she continued. Ana was glad for this clarity. The floral scent of the woman's perfume drifted into Ana's nose. She would have tried to pick out the name of the scent, being a perfume aficionado herself, but that wasn't the time. Some things could wait, and because the scent was nice, she made a mental note to remember the name.

"Uwe, can you remember that she used to give you sweets each time we visited," she said as she turned to her younger brother.

"I do," he said, looking up from his phone finally as though the memories had awakened him like a splash of cold water. Ana watched him slip the device into his pocket and reach for the picture as though he was seeing it for the first time.

Ana found herself smiling as his face lit up with a nostalgic smile. Ana knew Gabriella, the sexpert; she knew Gabriella, the sex-loving partner and wife to Bernd. What she didn't know and what she was just getting to know was that Gabriella and Bernd were the nice neighbors next door.

The woman stood up from the table, leaving the picture in her brother's hand, and walked back to her desk at the end of the room.

"You guys should come home with me," she said suddenly. "Let's have dinner together and talk about Gabriella and Bernd at my place," she said in a playful tone, yet Ana could tell that she wouldn't be entirely happy if she was turned down.

Ana wouldn't have said no; she wouldn't have refused, especially not after coming this far, but she needed to know if Andre would join her or if he wouldn't. He may have come with her to the office, but she also understood that he may have plans of his own. She turned to him, and just before she whispered her questions, he spoke.

"We would love to," he said. His enthusiasm confirmed that he was as ready as she was to visit the house of these strangers.

"It's about closing time," the woman said in a voice that sounded like a mother's as she gathered the scattered files on her table into a neat pile. Her brothers did the same, and in minutes, they all headed towards the large SUV parked at the front of the office.

●●●●●●●●

"I'm Joan, by the way," the woman said as they walked to the car.

Finally, she has a name, Ana thought. She had been wondering when she would know her name, and she had been hoping to achieve that feat without asking her.

Away from her thoughts, she saw Andre and the brothers ahead of them bonding as they chatted about the very hot summer and global warming like old friends. The thought of how connected everyone is, children of the same mother, siblings of one family, humanity, sauntered across Ana's mind. Around them, the sky was darkening, and light traffic was building up on the road beside them. Ana didn't need to check her watch to know that it was almost 7 p.m. and that they had spent more than one hour at the office.

"I'm Ana," Ana responded as they shook hands. Joan had removed her jacket, and she let it hang from the hand that held her bag. With the jacket off, Ana couldn't help but notice the slim figure that the ill-fitting jacket had been hiding as she walked beside her. It reminded her of anorexic models.

"So how did you know about Gabriella and her husband?" she asked Ana in a voice that was stripped free of suspicion. If anyone was looking at them, they would assume that they were probably long-lost friends or acquaintances that had run into each other after a long time.

Ana thought about the question, and like every time that she had thought about it, the discovery sounded ridiculous to her.

I stumbled on Gabriella's diary while going through a stranger's trash can. Ana thought no matter how ridiculous it sounded, it was the truth, and the only thing that had changed about it was that she now knew someone that knew the couple.

So, when she and Joan were settled in the car, she went over the tale of that day as she once did with Andre and Theo. As she spoke, she could hear Andre talking to the brothers about books, and not for the first time that day, she was glad that she had brought him along. Not just because she was more comfortable following the strangers home in his company, but because Andre was having the time of his life too.

"That's quite a tale," Joan said after Ana finished.

"It is," Ana answered.

For a while, Ana had expected to hear the words that she had materialized in her head as she spoke. She had never thought about it, but the possibility of the siblings asking her to hand over the diary existed as a thought in her head, especially with the relationship that they had with the couple. As the car slowed in front of the house, Joan remained quiet as though she was considering a similar possibility. Ana feared that she was thinking about that, and she began to prepare her response.

"I may have something that you will find absolutely interesting," Joan said as the car's engine stopped and her brothers hopped out.

Something that I will find interesting? Ana thought to herself. Her curiosity was piqued.

Ana looked at the house for the first time hoping to distract herself from the thought that the words had awakened.

"But let's get dinner first." Joan tapped Ana's knee gently and turned to open the door.

What can this possibly be? Ana wondered again.

"Sure, sure," Ana replied, and she followed Joan out of the car.

Dinner was a feast of vegetables and fruits.

"My bad...my bad," Joan had wailed as soon as she came out from the kitchen moments after they had all entered the house.

"I forgot to mention that we were having a fruit fast," she declared in the same regretful tone that made Ana think that the situation was worse than it really was. The sound of her hands slamming against her thighs almost made Ana jump from her seat. It felt dramatic, but Joan didn't seem like a dramatic person to her. She must be indeed serious, Ana concluded.

Ana felt as though she was in a spice market as the scent of different exotic spices surrounded them. And no matter how much she looked, she couldn't find the source of the intrusive spices. So, she did what she saw Andre doing; she leaned into the couch and enjoyed it.

"We could order Chinese for them or anything else they want," Uwe, the youngest brother, said as he flopped on the couch the way any lastborn would. It appeared that being in the home environment had changed his disposition from the semi-serious one to a very relaxed one. Ana looked around her, and she couldn't help but notice how the house looked so much like Joan. If there was one word that came readily to mind, it was minimalism. The living room looked more like the mix of a man cave and a naturalist's lair. The walls shimmered in bright white and were almost plain except for a vintage wall clock that hung just above a wide television screen. The living room area had only two long blue couches, and other than two long flute-like flower pots positioned at the ends of the room brimming with real palm trees, there was nothing else. Ana couldn't tell if she liked it or not; all she knew was that it looked so much like Joan did—no unnecessary adornment, no ostentatious display.

Ana wasn't hungry. If there was any hunger she felt, any desire that needed to be met, it was the information that Joan had promised her.

What could it possibly be? she wondered for the umpteenth time. She hoped that she would not burst with anticipation.

"Don't bother," she said as she looked from brother to sister, and just like she hoped, Andre was in support of her.

"We are fine with whatever you guys are having," he said. She knew a lot about Andre to know that he would rather not eat. They had known each other for months before he ever ate any of Flora's food that she brought to work. But she also knew how sensitive he was. He was wise enough to know that turning down a host's hospitality was akin to insult.

"It wouldn't take time," said Eric from a narrow corridor that led to the kitchen. In his hands was a platter filled with an assortment of grapes and berries.

"I insist on having whatever you are serving... who would turn down an opportunity for a body system cleanse?" Ana rambled. Her mouth had watered a little at the sight of the fruits. It reminded her of how long it had been since she last ate a piece of fruit.

"I concur." Andre raised his hand in a mock voting gesture.

"So, fruit it is," Joan said with a smile of relief. Ana couldn't help but smile too.

Maybe we'll eventually become friends, Ana wondered.

The fruit arrived in large platters—bunches of fresh bananas surrounded by clusters of ripe cherries whose mouthwatering scent hit their noses before the platter got to them. The purple grapes looked so fresh that Ana couldn't help but imagine the flavors bursting in her mouth. There were strawberries and dazzling blueberries that formed a picturesque sight fit for photographing and posting on Instagram.

"Is this Germany or the courts of a roman goddess?" Andre teased as he stared greedily at the platter that Joan set between them on the couch. The scent of fruits and spices wafted into Ana's nostrils, and she wished that she could imprint that scent in her nose forever.

"You can call it both," Joan replied with a wink. They all erupted into peals of uproarious laughter, and for a while, Ana almost believed the fairy tale that the entire scenario resembled. Anyone who had walked in on them would have believed that they probably were family or even close friends.

When the laughter had died down, Joan mentioned with a noticeable trace of nostalgia in her voice, "Gabriella nurtured my love of fruit."

"True... true... true," Eric grunted, his mouth filled with cherries. He wiped away a solitary trail of the cherry juice dripping down his chin with the paper towels that were tucked underneath the platter as soon as Ana's eyes met his. Andre and Uwe were distracted by the program playing on the TV.

And then the moment that Ana had been waiting for began. As they feasted on the fruits and the chilled water that Joan had brought from the kitchen, Ana and Andre listened to the interesting tale of Gabriella and Bernd's lives from the lips of the siblings that had grown up with them.

•••••••••

Ana sat gingerly at the edge of her bed, her feet nestled in the once-fluffy carpet. It was late, well past midnight, and the sky beyond her window was filled with stars, and everywhere was quiet except for the familiar sounds of nighttime—a few chirping insects, the sound of a solitary car en route to its destination, creaking furniture. Apart from this, everywhere was as quiet as a silent night.

She should have been asleep, considering all the excitement from the day and how busy the next day would be, but she wasn't. Ana knew that there was no way that she would sleep soon, especially not with the memories replaying in her head and the envelope in her hands.

"After they left suddenly," Joan had said, moments after she had described how much Gabriella and Bernd had cared for them as though they were their own kids. "We were so sad... all of us."

Ana recalled the way she had gestured to her brothers, who both nodded half-heartedly. At that point, one thing was sure for Ana, Joan was the spokesperson of the trio. It was she who spoke of their individual and shared experiences; it was she who described Bernd as gentle and Gabriella as a people person. All her brothers ever did was nod in acquiescence, Eric still munching on his fruits, paying more attention than Uwe.

"I knew what they did, their line of work... I was the one who told my brothers and eventually our parents about it when they disappeared."

Ana tried again to imagine the situation, the younger siblings, and what they probably understood about the jobs and lives of their favorite loving tenants. Joan seemed to her like the precocious kind who would have understood, perhaps Eric also did, but she doubted if Uwe had. She wanted to ask, but she didn't want anything to stop Joan from completing the story.

Still on the edge of her bed, her finger rubbing against the back of the envelope as though she was undecided about opening it, she recalled how Joan had told her how the couple had left suddenly without coming back for their belongings.

Joan had excused herself and left Ana alone with the men and Andre, who were watching a talk show by some famous reality star, before coming back with a stack of brown envelopes. "You know they kept on sending letters," Joan said as she walked to the couch and sat beside Ana.

"Letters?" Ana remembered asking; her voice had quivered with surprise and excitement. Surprise because she had just told her how they had disappeared suddenly. People who disappeared in that manner hardly sent traceable mail; it was dangerous, stupid even. Maybe they had their reasons, she concluded. And then there was the excitement that she felt because she realized that whatever was in those envelopes could well be a clue that was missing from the diary. Whatever it was, Ana could remember how she couldn't wait to see what those letters were about.

Ana could also remember how the scent of fruits and old stationery had wafted into her nostrils as soon as Joan sat beside her, and she couldn't help but imagine her pulling out the letters from the bottom of a box stored in some attic.

"Because the letters had no return address, we couldn't reply to them, and because they continued to pay the rent, we assumed that they would come back." Ana remembered how Joan had tied her errant blond tresses into a bun and how her voice had quivered wistfully.

"What was in the mail?" Ana found herself asking the question that had been crawling around her insides like a crab trying to climb out of a hole.

"A lot... but I will let you find out yourself," Joan had replied with a shrug, and just as Ana had hoped, she reached out and handed them over to her. Ana wasn't the religious type; she didn't believe in miracles; she only believed in magic, the sort of magic that could only happen in books like *Harry Potter* and *Lord of The Rings*. That was her limit. Anything other than that was simply over-the-top tricks. But she could have sworn that magic was what happened when her hands wrapped around the stack of mail. She could have sworn she felt a shiver run through her body. So, she nodded that she understood. This must have been the thing that Joan had promised her when they were in the car.

"The letters stopped coming after a while, and we feared the worse," Joan said after gulping a mouthful of water.

"That they had died?" Ana asked, her heart skipping a beat as she waited for Joan's answer. Even in that moment, on the edge of her bed, as she recalled the conversation that had ensued hours ago, Ana still felt a similar reaction.

"One thing we noticed was that soon they started putting addresses on the letters, and that itself kept on," Joan added as she clasped her hands in her lap as though the act of reliving that part of their past was taking something from her.

Ana nodded in understanding. Parts of the puzzle seemed to be falling into place. If they had indeed continued seeing people as she had read in the diary so far, the possibility of the police visiting again was very likely. And the sudden disappearance also made sense to her.

"We thought that they had died when their rent payments stopped," Joan said as she stretched her leg in front of her.

Ana remembered how Joan's eyes had misted as she told her about the days of waiting and hoping. And Ana could remember how her hand had slid to Joan's hands in a surprising move of tenderness and how she had said "I'm sorry" to her.

"This was the first letter from them... you should start from this one," Joan had said in response to Ana's question about how to read the letters.

"After all these years, we finally decided to put the house up for sale because we need money for some urgent family problem," Joan said, and Ana couldn't help but hear the regret in her voice. That seemed like days ago, but it was only hours ago, late in the evening.

And on that quiet night, as Ana flipped open the envelope and pulled out the once white letter that had begun to soften and grow brown in some parts, she felt her heart racing in anticipation. Under the light of her bedside lamp, she began reading.

Dear Joan, Eric, and Uwe... if you are reading this mail, it means that you already know that we have disappeared.

10: THE LETTERS

Ana did something that she wouldn't normally do, especially when she had something interesting to read. As soon as she read the first line of the first letter in the stack that Joan had handed to her, she stopped. The letter wasn't just an interesting book, it wasn't even a book, but she had never felt connected to anything the way she was to it. And she knew herself; she could end up reading anything, the entire stack, even if it was that interesting.

I may not stop if I start, so I had better control myself, she thought to herself. And with that, she picked up her phone and set a timer for thirty minutes. She would read as much as she could in thirty minutes and continue when she got back from work later that day. That was the deal.

Earlier, she had contemplated taking the mail to the office and reading it with Andre during their lunch break, especially because she had arrived home late, but she had fallen for the temptation. She had fallen into the trap of an uncontrollable desire to read the letters.

She had barely touched the food that she had sneaked up to her room. Her belly was still filled with the fruit that she had eaten at Joan's. But she had ensured that she had her water bottle filled with cool water.

"Thirty minutes," she whispered before she picked up the letter again and began from the beginning as the time on her phone changed from 01:59 to 2:00 a.m.

Dear Joan, Eric, and Uwe, if you are reading this letter, it means that you already know that we have disappeared. I am sorry that we had to leave that way, that we had to part ways without saying goodbye. It wasn't planned, and I'm sure you can already guess what happened. I hope to tell you about that in my next letter to you. But with that out of the way, I'd love to know how you all are. I am very sure that you all are fine and in good health. We are also. Bernd says hello. As I write you this letter, my feet are in his lap, and his hands are massaging them so well. And I would have shut my eyes to enjoy this moment if I wasn't writing. So, if you really want to know how I feel at the moment. I feel so good. Ana couldn't help but smile. The picture of how the siblings and Gabriella's relationship really was had begun to make sense to her, and she discovered that she liked it, loved it even. Perhaps because it reminded her of how she was that kid who enjoyed the company of older folks. And without taking her eyes off the letter, she returned to the line where she had stopped and continued.

Dear Joan, I know we had plans. Lots of plans, I must say. I know that I promised to teach you many things the last time you visited. I am sorry that I couldn't do that before I left. I very much wanted to fulfill my promise, but I just couldn't, and I hope that someday I will be able to teach you, or perhaps I will send it in a letter. Only I know that it won't be the same. I won't be able to see your intelligent eyes light up as you digest and learn the new things that I will teach you or hear you say, "Oh, wow, that is amazing."

Did I tell you that those are some of the best things I love about you—your enthusiasm and your sense of wonder? Please do not ever lose those.

I imagine you are all wondering where we are and if we are doing well. Once again, I assure you that we are, but I will not tell you where we are. I cannot.

Ana exhaled. She tried to picture Gabriella writing the letter in a cramped room with boarded-up windows or in a motel room that they had both rented under false names. It was the same way people on the run in the movies or mystery books did. She tried to imagine her trying to be cheerful despite all she was feeling. What would possibly make one cheerful, especially when one is on the run like a fugitive. Ana had no answer for that question, so she continued reading.

I really don't know what to say, and even Bernd doesn't. Sometimes words just aren't enough. But maybe if I start by trying to tell you about my day today, I will find the right things to say to you eventually. You know it is not only a journey of a thousand miles that begins with one step; everything else begins with a first trial.

So, this is how my day started today. I don't know if I should be telling you this, but I woke up to a kiss from Bernd. Maybe when you grow older and fall in love, you will understand what it means to be awoken by the kiss of your lover. It feels like sunshine to a plant; it feels like water to dry soil. It is everything, and it was the best part of my morning.

So, with that done, we both sat and talked about all the things that we needed to talk about, you know, adult stuff.

Just as I have always told you, the secret to the success of any and every relationship is communication. I know you once argued that it was love. Well, I thought that I should remind you again that even love suffers when communication is missing.

It doesn't matter what the relationship is like. It could be a friendship or something more; both partners must learn to communicate their feelings, communicate about their plans, fears, and anything. I had never realized how important that was up until now. If myself and Bernd have ever been close, those moments are little compared to this moment. It is true what they say; it is moments like this that really bring out the best or worst of people. For us, I must say, it has indeed brought out the best in us.

After we were done with that, I got up and made us each a cup of coffee, which we had with the leftover bread and butter from the previous day.

I know what you are thinking now. I can hear your voice saying, "Gabriella didn't you brush before eating?"

Well, I didn't, but I will still brush my teeth. I always do. The routine of our lives had changed since the day we left the house, since the day we fled from the city, but only the routine had changed. Everything else is still the same. I still brush my teeth and take care of myself like I taught you guys, only I do it much later. I doubt if you guys understand.

So, after our breakfast, we talk again about our plans for the day. We do a lot of talking nowadays. That's what I get for being stuck in a place with the love of my life, with my best friend.

That reminds me, guys, if and when the time comes to fall in love, please ensure that you fall in love with your best friend.

So back to how my day went. If I was back at the house, you all pretty well know how my day goes, how our day goes (especially in the early days).

Since we have all the time (at least I do), perhaps I should remind you how my days go.

Most mornings, after I wake up, which is always as early as six am, I always prepare coffee first, especially during winter. We are coffee people, myself and Bernd. After the coffee, I pull out my daily planner and check out my plans for the day while Bernd brushes his teeth and showers.

As soon as I am done with my planner, I make breakfast for both of us, and I brush my teeth and have my bath. We always take breakfast together, even now. Of all that has changed, this hasn't changed.

Bernd goes to his garden as soon as he is done while I prepare myself for any visitors that I have scheduled for the day. I attend to each visitor till 7 p.m., and most times, Bernd joins us (if necessary). You have experienced days like this when you visited. So, it is definitely not new to you.

As soon as the last visitor leaves, myself and Bernd prepare dinner together, have showers, and settle to eat. I always tell people that come to me with their marital problems about this. Nothing bonds a couple together than the times that they spend together. Somedays, Bernd doesn't do anything, he only watches me as I work, and the fact that he is with me is often as effective as he cooking with me.

On some days, we watch movies together before falling asleep on the couch or heading to the bedroom as soon as either of us begins to doze. On other days, I regale him with tales of my day. Yet again, this is one of our best moments together. Talking about the fun moments of my day, laughing so loud and so hard that tears stream from our eyes as we do that.

Things are different now. Even if we are mostly together now, we can no longer laugh as hard as we once did.

Ana felt her eyes cloud with tears. She folded the letter in two as her chest heaved. It almost felt as though she was reading the diary. The emotions, the feelings that all she read evoked in her were almost too much, but she couldn't stop. She exhaled yet again and continued with the next letter.

Things are different now, and even if Bernd is super supportive as he always is, it just feels different being in the same place all day. We cannot receive visitors anymore; Bernd can no longer go out to his garden. Somedays, I see that look on his face, and I can tell that he misses the garden as much as I miss the spacious kitchen, the wide living room, the comfort of our bed, our roomy shower, the scent of Bernd's clothes when he returns from work. I miss your monthly visits; I miss all the questions that you guys always ask me and the meals that I would prepare whenever you guys were around. But you know what? I am grateful still.

Everything here feels so small, and you know what I miss the most? I miss helping people. I can't help but think about the many people that will have no one to talk to, no one to share their burdens with. It feels like I have lost an arm. So last week I decided that I will write them letters. Bernd wasn't sure it was a good idea at first, but I was able to convince him. I told him that I will not put a return address to prevent the trouble that he feared. He agreed, and that's why I am sending you guys this first letter. Please help us tell your parents that we are fine and that we will continue paying the rent as we hope to come back.

Love you guys, G and B.

The tears finally rolled down Ana's face as she folded the paper back into its permanently folded shape and slid it into the envelope. She hastily wiped it off as though someone else was watching her, only no one was. She just couldn't imagine herself crying. She felt it was too childish, and she knew that Flora had warned her against thinking such thoughts. "Only psychopaths and non-living things don't cry," she once told her.

She looked at her phone and realized that the timer had rung. She had been too engrossed in the contents of the letter that she hadn't heard it ring.

She stood up to stretch and stepped into the toilet to relieve herself. She could feel her eyes heavy, but it wasn't as heavy as her heart. One thing she was sure of is that she would certainly dream about Bernd and Gabriella in the few hours that she had left to sleep before dawn.

•••••••

Ana half listened and half read, and between these two activities, she spooned her food into her mouth. It was her favorite meal, but it tasted more like a watery gruel, and she would have dumped it if not for the growls in her belly. Aside from the feasts of fruits that she had in Joan's house the day before, she had eaten nothing. She had returned her lunch back to the fridge, and she knew that she had Flora to answer to when she got back home later that day, and she already knew what she would tell her.

"So, are you telling me that these letters are like a substitute for the missing pages of the diary?" Andre asked her. His eyes were fixated on hers hungrily. She had noticed it the last time that they were together. His enthusiasm about Gabriella's life was also increasing.

At least I'm not the only addicted one, she had thought to herself, but she said nothing to him. She knew that Andre would never agree to that, and even if he would, she wasn't in the mood to tell him.

"Yes," she answered casually. *But I just told you that now,* she wanted to add annoyingly. She was grumpy, and her grumpiness made his questions seem more annoying than they actually were.

Her eyes hurt so much as though they held grains of sand in them. She had barely slept for four out of the seven hours that she usually slept, and even her sleep had been distorted with dreams, several dreams.

In one of them, she had found herself on the run in a dark alley with several footsteps ricocheting behind her. No matter how hard she ran, she found out that she couldn't outrun her pursuers, and they finally caught up with her. And just before she leaped out of her skin in that dream-like state, she saw that her pursuers were Gabriella and Bernd. And moments later, she realized that they weren't even her pursuers. They also were on the run, and heavy footfalls sounded behind the three of them. She couldn't tell if she had woken up or if another dream had continued afterward, but she was certain that there was another, perhaps two more. But by the time her alarm woke her up, she was not only grumpy, but her thoughts were as squiggly and jumbled as the two earphones tangled in her bag.

"I don't know, but it seems that their story gets more interesting at every point," Andre interrupted her attempt to go back to reading. Ana exhaled. It was better than telling Andre off. She might be on the verge of screaming at him, but she also realized that their break periods were often spent gossiping and eating, and Andre was making casual conversation as he always does.

"Well, I have noticed that also," Ana replied and contemplated folding the letter back into its envelope.

Around them, the library cafeteria was busy but not distractingly noisy. Ana had learned a long time ago to tune out ambient noises. So, the shuffle of feet, the mumbling voices, the clink of cutlery against plates, and occasional laughter around them didn't bother her.

She decided to read just part of the letter with the few minutes left in their break period, and to do that, she knew that she would have to ask for Andre's permission.

"Andre, darling," she said in her I-have-a-favor-to-ask voice after folding the letter and placing it on the table beside her plate of food, which she had abandoned. Multitasking was her thing, but this wasn't working in her favor at that moment. Perhaps it had to do with how much she wanted to find out what was contained in this new letter. The hunger for that did supersede the one for food or because she felt that reading would calm her down. Whatever the case, she wanted to do just one thing, and that one thing was to read the letters undisturbed.

"What is it?" Andre lifted his brow suspiciously, knowing that he wouldn't like whatever came after those words or with the rub of Ana's hands on his downturned hand on the table.

"Can I read for ten minutes, and then we talk for five minutes?" Ana asked in a childish voice. Her eyes locked on Andre's own as she looked out for his reaction.

"Girl, just tell me that I have been disturbing you," he said with mock anger, pulling out his hand from underneath hers. He turned his body away from her and sucked his teeth as though he was genuinely hurt.

"It's not like that," Ana replied as she made to pull him back towards her, but the table between them made that impossible, so she gave up.

"Well, go ahead with your reading," he said, "there's a cute boy I need to attend to in my DMs," he said as he looked from her to his phone. He winked at her as though he meant something other than what he had just said.

Ana looked at him with that tell-me-about-it look that friends as close as them share as their secret code. Andre waved her look away as though indicating that she would hear nothing about what he was up to. But both of them knew that it was only a matter of time before he began to spill all. He sipped from his smoothie and swallowed what was left of his vegetable pie. Unlike Ana, his appetite was ravenous.

"So, we both get the gist of each other," she teased him, and they both took that as a cue that meant they should each face their own concerns.

Ana picked up the letter from where it was and began reading it again from the beginning.

Dear Joan, Eric, and Uwe.

How are you guys? I trust that you are all doing well. I cannot say that for ourselves because it has been a tough few weeks for us; perhaps I should call it the toughest weeks of our lives. Because that is what it is.

I had thought that I would be able to send a letter every two weeks, but that doesn't seem possible. I wouldn't have been able to send this one if I hadn't promised that I would share some things with you all in the last letter.

In the last month alone, we have moved from place to place at least thrice. I feel sad about it and extremely inconvenient most especially, but as always, Bernd has been there for me. He had been, for me, a pillar of support, a beacon in these dark nights, a shelter in these moments. He says that I am the brave one, but I doubt if I am brave, I doubt if I am as brave as he is. But then I agree. It takes bravery to wake up and believe in a new day; it takes bravery to send this letter because I promised you that I would. It takes bravery to want to help people, even if I am the one that needs help.

The challenges of the past month have reminded me of the weeks before we disappeared from the house. And each time I remember those dark days, I shudder.

I doubt if I ever told you about the first day that the police came.

They were four that day. Four stern-looking men dressed in their uniforms. Even if they weren't rude and raucous, the sight of the men in our house was as scary as the sight of an incoming lion on a person's path.

They asked questions about my line of work, they wanted to know how I made money. I showed them all the documents of my inheritance. I could sense their unbelief, yet I could also sense their confusion. Whatever they were looking for was nowhere to be found. And because of that, they had no choice but to leave us. The days that followed that day were the toughest. I suspected every sound. I feared for every strange movement. A seemingly harmless knock on our door always made my heart drop to my knees. Fear dictated and directed the order of my life. It influenced anything and everything that I (and, indeed, we) did. There were nights that I couldn't sleep, and days I expected them to show up. But those days soon passed.

Ana paused. She folded the letter in half. She didn't know if she indeed felt thirsty or if she just wanted to take a moment to take all the information in, but she drank water. Yet the coolness of the water that slid down her throat did very little to calm her body down. Seated across from her at the table was Andre, who was engrossed with messaging his potential love interest.

Nice one, she thought as she realized that she still had time to herself.

Her heart throbbed a little faster than normal, and sweat broke out on her scalp. Ana knew what was happening; it always happened to her, especially whenever she feels drawn into the world of whatever she's reading. She tried to recall the word that she had once heard. The word describes the process of experiencing the feeling of others. It began with a "v" and rhymed with the word "serious." She finally remembered after the third try. The word was "vicarious." She could feel the experience of Gabriella and Bernd vicariously, and she wondered how they had coped in those days. She tapped at her phone's screen and realized that there was still time to read more, so she flipped open the letter and continued from where she stopped.

We had thought that those days had passed, and soon I began receiving visitors. Although we were careful, me and the visitors, and the visits continued. You guys have said it before (especially you, Joan), and it is so true; nothing makes me happier than helping people.

I can remember the first person that came was a woman, and I can remember how excited I was when she told me about the results of what I recommended for her. Others followed, the young students, the older men, women who no longer feel confident in their bodies, newlyweds. They came alone, they came as a result of recommendation, and none of them ever left the same. Life seemed perfect despite the scare of the police until that day.

An exhale and a gulp of water later, and Ana continued. She knew then that the grip of the story in the letter, coupled with the dry weather, was responsible for her thirst.

It all began with a phone call, a strange phone call. If I can remember, I was returning from the kitchen, where I had just finished cleaning up the dishes, when I heard the phone ring.

I hurried to go pick up the call with hands still wet. The voice that I heard was the voice of a stranger. The words that came out of his mouth were simple, but they made me shiver afterward. "The police are coming again, and this time, they will make you both disappear even if they find nothing." And the line went dead. For a while, I found myself asking the dead phone who the caller was and waiting for the answer. I must have been in shock. After I recovered, my mind began to spin like a wheel as different possibilities sprung up. Yet there was one question that had no answer—who was the caller?

Other questions came afterward, questions such as Was the caller a friend? Was he one of my customers? Were we being watched? Have they found any evidence?

The call had been too short for me to even attempt to imagine who the caller might be. And I couldn't even tell if it was my mind or if it was indeed real, but it felt as though

I could remember the caller's heavy breath, his urgency, but most importantly—the words.

Luckily and unluckily for me, I had no clients and no visitors that day. I considered it lucky because I doubted if I would have been able to attend to them as I should have. I always want my visitors to see how much of a human that I am, but I don't think I want them to see me in the state that I was in on that day.

Unluckily, being alone and scared is one of the worst combinations. I knew then that if I had someone to talk to, I would have felt better. But there was no one, and the only person that I wanted to talk to was Bernd, but he was at work, and I didn't want to disturb him. So, I spent the rest of that day thinking, fearing, and waiting. And trust me, that day was the longest day of my life. The afternoon stretched so long that it felt like a week instead of just a few hours. I usually snacked during the afternoons, but my appetite had disappeared; it vanished like candlelight in the wind. And several times, I imagined going to call Bernd, but I withheld myself.

I spilled all to him as soon as he came, and it was then, several hours after the strange phone call, the flood of tears broke out like waters from a dam, and I wept. Bernd held me in his strong arms. He whispered how that everything would be fine and that he would ensure that nothing would happen to me, but it seemed at that moment that words of comfort which were usually enough for me, weren't enough. I wanted something tangible, something permanent. But what it was, I couldn't tell, so I settled for the words of comfort.

Ana exhaled again and flipped to the reverse side of the letter.

The next morning, I woke up to Bernd's arms around me and his voice whispering in my ears. "We will leave tonight," he said with an air of finality. My body stiffened; my breath caught in my throat.

"Leave?" I asked him as though I didn't understand what the word meant. "Yes, leave," he replied. "We will run away this night."

Like a confused person, I turned to face him and bombarded him with questions. "Where would we run to? What do we pack? Who can we stay with?"

Some of the questions made sense, others didn't, but I didn't care. I was afraid and confused.

As you may have noticed, we left everything as though we had just gone for a walk or a trip to the park. It was Bernd's suggestion. He told me to take just what we needed—toiletries, a few clothes, and money. According to him, we couldn't tell if we were being watched, and we also didn't want anything to slow us down if we were being pursued.

We left that night armed with only a handbag and the hope of an incident-free escape. I will not write in this letter where we went. But we went as far away from the region as we could under cover of darkness. We took buses, and in the morning, we boarded the train. When we arrived at our first destination, we felt utmost relief, yet the fear still gnawed at the edges of our minds. Fear still made us jerk awake at night at the sounds of mice scurrying around on the roof; it made us look around us on the street. You know (or maybe you don't) fear is such a terrible thing. It is like a chain that binds you, a leash that controls you, a bit, and a bridle that restrains you. Fear did all of this to us.

We stayed in our first location for weeks, and there was no incident at all. I even began sending letters to a few of my trusted friends and customers, and just the way I included in yours, I told them not to tell anyone if they were asked about us. We told them we were fine, and we even attended to a few by mail. We would have remained there a long time if Bernd hadn't noticed the strange men that seemed to be watching where we stayed. At first, he thought nothing about it, but when he saw the same men the next day, he told me that we had to leave, and so we left.

And it has been almost the same situation—us moving, them following. That is why I haven't been able to send the letters as I promised to. I have to go now, and I don't know if and when I will be able to write you guys again, but if I find the time, place, and the peace of mind, I will write you more. As always, Bernd says hello. I hope you guys are reading your books and learning about the world around you as much as you can.

Love, G and B

11: MORE

If there was something that Ana loved most about the weekend, it was time. Time that allowed her to stay as long as she loved, wrapped between the sheets, caught up in the warm embrace of her comforter. Or in the wonderful world of fiction on the days she read. Weekends meant that she had all the time to decide if she should get up or not despite the intrusive sun's ray or her pesky alarms. Flora knew better than to disturb her.

On weekdays, her days often began before sunrise. By sunrise, she was either having breakfast or about to head out.

Much more than time, she realized that what she loved most about weekends was freedom. The freedom to break out of the routine that her daily life was structured around.

Her room was already bathed in the sun's rays that had managed to slip past the spaces between her old curtains.

Parts of the house were quiet, but she could hear the sound of activities on the street—the roar of automobiles, the drone of televisions or radios, and the yelling of an agitated child.

But none of these sounds bothered her. With her legs stretched out in front of her and her back pressed against the headboard, she picked up the diary from her bag.

The scent of her perfume had already replaced that of old paper and dust that the diary had smelled like when she first picked it up. What was she expecting? The diary had become like a part of her body. It had spent more days in her bag than any book she had ever read. She hated books being in her bag, especially if they were not hardcovers. The sight of curled edges, brown tips, or creases always annoyed her. She could always tell if any of the users had left the borrowed books in their bags from these signs. To avoid this, she always had to choose between her desire to go along with that favorite book of hers or leave it on her bedside table.

Her finger slid through page after page as she looked for the last page she stopped at. The bookmark must have fallen in her bag. The sound of flipping pages was dulled because of the softness of the diary's pages.

"One of the things I love about books," a vlogger had said on one of his podcast recordings, "is the sound of paper sliding against paper. That, along with the scent of a book, the hardness of the spine, the smoothness of the cover." Ana could remember how she had smiled as she listened to the podcast on her way to work. She could relate to most of what was mentioned. And even if the diary didn't fit into all these qualities, she knew that it had its special quality. On the days she thought about it, she could remember that she now associated it with the feeling of old leather, the scent of old books, and the beauty of Gabriella's almost calligraphic handwriting. And there was something else.

Since she began reading the letters, the restlessness that she once felt, especially when she discovered that the couple was being hunted, seemed to have disappeared. Like parts of a puzzle that had slid into place, the information from the letters filled in the blank spaces in the diary.

She placed the parts of the diary that fell out as she flipped the brown pages.

She may have read those parts, but she couldn't allow any part of the diary to go missing—not on her watch. She had read books where regular people became custodians of certain secrets found in books—a shy girl stumbling upon a witch's grimoire, a quirky scientist stumbling upon the works of Nostradamus. These discoveries often become life-changing events for the characters. She felt she now belonged in such leagues. Only she realized that if there was any superpower to be had from having the diary, it was being knowledgeable about sex and sexual matters. The thought filled her face with a bright smile.

"Fixing sexual matters isn't the only thing Gabriella is good at; she is also a fantastic writer," Andre had mentioned one day when Ana was reading the letters beside him. He had picked up one randomly, and pulled it out of its envelope gently, the way he had seen her do. The remains of their lunch were pushed to the edge of the table, their hands and lips wiped clean with the crumpled tissue paper on their plates. Andre had glanced through the letter, but unlike her, he was more fascinated with the writing and the intrigue than the content or message. Whenever they were together, they always seemed cocooned from the others in the cafeteria.

"Yes. She has some of the best handwriting that I have ever seen," Ana had remarked without lifting her eyes from the letter she was reading. It was the day she remembered telling Andre that she wished that they survived the communist police, and if wishes really came to pass, her wish would be to meet the couple.

The blue tick of her pen revealed the part that she had read last. And as she always did before reading any book or material, Ana placed her finger on the first word and began.

I could call today a pretty normal day. And it really was, except for one interesting visit that I had.

The second visitor of the day had barely left when I heard the knock. I assumed he had left something behind. Because the last visitor looked like that sort of person. The sort of person whose mind is never settled on a particular thing. Even before he told me, I had noticed it as soon as he sat down. You know it is possible to know how someone is from just a glance at their face. His eyes darted around the store like a bee moving from one flower to the other. If he hadn't told me who had recommended him, I would have suspected that he was a thief or a government agent. But all that changed when I asked him what the matter was.

My girlfriend says that I have changed. He blurted out. In that moment, nothing held his attention as much as my face. He had looked at me, not in shame, not in fear, but in desperation.

His problem, as I later discovered, was a case of a lack of attention. I discovered that he was one of those individuals that lacked an ability to fixate on something/anything for a long time—even sex.

I remember telling Bernd about it later at night as I shared about all the parts of my day. His arms were wrapped around me, our bodies still a little moist from our time in the shower. This was moments after he had told me about his day. We had both laughed when he mentioned how that could never be his problem. "With how hot you are and with how crazy I am about you. Nothing can distract me from you, not even for a second." The words ended with his lips pressed on the side of my neck.

Well, I told "Mr. darting eyes" what to do and gave him the necessary toys that would save his relationship. Of course, just like everyone who visits, his face was a mask of joy and excitement. His darting eyes and roaming attention had begun again, and I had to whisk him away. So, I assumed that he was the one who came back.

I answered the door at the third knock with a frown on my face. Over the years, I have had a lot of people visit me both at the shop and at home, from strangers that never come back to friends that always come back. It wasn't Mr. darting eyes as I had thought. I was partly relieved. Standing there in the plainest dress that I have ever seen— a grey below-the-knee dress that seemed large enough to fit people twice the size of the wearer.

Blonde hair dropped to her shoulders like the tassels on a loafer, palm leaves on a tree. Some of that hair covered a part of her face. Her eyes were large but beautiful and adorned with some of the finest lashes that I have ever seen on a person. But I doubted if she knew that about herself.

For a while, we both stared at each other. Both of us taking in each other as though we were undecided about our next action. It was barely a minute, but it felt as though we spent an eternity in that weird silence.

I was the one who broke the ice first. Isn't that the saying people use? Breaking the ice, shattering the silence that boxed us in.

With a smile plastered on my face, I asked a question that was part question, part tease.

"Will you come in, or will we stare at each other all day?" She apologized in a voice that sounded timid and almost afraid. Her eyes fell to her feet as though I wasn't looking at her. I would have assumed that she was a child, a teenager of some sort.

Moments later, she was settled in one of the couches reserved for visitors in my sex shop. My sex shop is designed like a home and an office. The only things that make it seem official are the vials, jars, and toys that hung on the wall, beside charts and pictures. Other than that, every bit of it was homey as any of our homes. The walls are painted in the coolest and most relaxing shades of blue. Some of the past patients had commented that the ambiance of the shop had been very relaxing for them. I always tell them that to get a good result, it is always needful to be deliberate about everything that you do. Whether it is to get your partner to pay attention to you or to communicate to your partner that you would want to take your sex life to another level. Whatever it is, I always tell them, always remember to pay attention to the smallest detail. Apart from the wall paint, the chairs are mostly roomy couches that allow my guests to feel very relaxed. Hard chairs always make people uneasy and uncomfortable. Then there is the scent of herbs and spices that makes my office smell like a garden of fresh flowers. People have asked me why I put in all these efforts. And for every question, my answer has been the same. I care about everyone that walks into my shop. It has never been about profit for me but about giving value back. My biggest payment is and always has been the satisfied smiles on my clients' faces.

So back to the visitor, who introduced herself as Mary in that same voice that was barely louder than a whisper. It was summer, so I presented her with a choice between iced tea, water, or juice. Just as I suspected, she settled for water. Most people go for water. Whatever problems that brought them to my shop were often too much of a worry for them that anything else would seem like a frivolity.

If I had been wrong about her being one of the least confident persons I had ever seen, she confirmed it further.

I always try not to prejudge most of my visitors, but I could tell that whatever Mary's problem was, it had to do with self-esteem. My smile was the warmest, my voice the softest, but even from where she sat, she couldn't hold my gaze.

"My thirty-third birthday is in two days, yet I am a virgin. That was her response to my question about what had brought her to my shop. Her water was abandoned on the arm of the chair. She had mentioned the word "virgin" as though it was a curse, a vile disease.

No one finds me attractive. From where I sat watching her, listening to her like I listened to everyone with a face free of judgment, I could see how much she believed in her unattractiveness. There was a time in my life when I would have thought that her case was the worst case. But that was a long time ago.

Ana let out a deep breath. She ignored the smell of her morning breath or the crustiness at the corners of her eyes. It was the weekend, after all, and her parents weren't at home to intrude into this cocoon of freedom that she was enjoying. A wistful smile played out on her face as she marked the space above the last sentence with a blue star.

It always fascinated her how much of a storyteller Gabriella was. She recalled one of the courses on storytelling that she had taken in college. The lecturer had mentioned how the best storytellers were the most detailed people. They include all the details in their environments when telling a story. She remembered how they had all tittered when the lecturer had said, "If the wall that you are writing about is white, let your reader know. If your pulse races so fast that it sounds in your ears, say it, show it." And that is what she noticed about reading Gabriella's diary. Gabriella told everything as it was, every minor detail.

Ana's eyes traveled from the pile of clothes at the foot of her bed to the untidy shoe rack. She might have all the time and freedom during weekends, but she knew that if she didn't want Flora to arrange her room for her, she would have to do it herself. She thought about stopping at this point, at the point where her blue pen had marked the diary's page, but like an addict in need of a fix, she knew that she just couldn't. And just like she had at the beginning, she brought her finger to the last sentence.

But it was a long time ago.

I wasn't surprised that she had said that people considered her unattractive. I would have come to the same conclusion if I was a male, and if I wasn't trained in the manner that I am now.

"My parents want me to get married before the year is over, but I don't even have a boyfriend." Her voice rose to a loud pitch; her eyes revealed how painful her situation was, how desperate she wanted an answer. I listened and watched.

I know most people say it, but I wonder if people understand it as much as they say it. Men fall in love with their eyes, but women do so with their ears. Men will notice an attractive lady before they notice the one who sounds bright. I knew that Mary would be able to tell me this, but I could also tell that she didn't have an understanding of it.

The more I listened to her, the more I saw her beauty. One thing I know about beauty is that beauty is an inside job. If one doesn't feel beautiful inside, it would be hard for it to show outside. And that was the case with Mary.

Beyond her ill-fitting clothes and her seemingly unkempt hair was a beauty so stunning that it seemed as though I hadn't seen someone like her ever. A few questions later, I got the answer to what I suspected was her problem:

"I was the only child for years until my parents had another child. As soon as my younger sister arrived, it seemed as though I had been a placeholder for years. They lavished her with so much love and attention. And it seemed as though for every flood of attention and love that she got, all I got in return was just a few drops. Soon those drops stopped coming."

Her words flowed, and her voice got louder. It felt as though she hadn't had any conversation in years, and like a dam that had finally found an outlet, she let it all out.

"Everyone is beautiful." Those were the first words I told her. Her furrowed brows and stretched lips showed that she doubted me. Like the moment when we first met, I let another silence settle over us.

I told her what I tell most of my skeptical visitors. And this is it. "Before I give you anything to consume or use, I will give you the most important thing first." She watched me seated across from her, separated by nothing but the distance between our couches. Her look said it all. What can I possibly give her other than sex toys and sex tips?

Self-belief. I watched her mouth part as though she needed an intake of breath. Her brows furrowed again, and she adjusted her frame within her oversize dress. From the contours, I could tell that she had a beautiful body, the kind men salivate about. But no man would have the patience to look at her more than once.

My voice became sterner, and I told her that if she wasn't ready to believe me, she could leave.

Moments later, I watched tears travel down her face as I told her how her lack of belief in herself was what had made her believe that she was unattractive. I began to list the features that I noticed about her—her pretty eyes with the hooded lashes, her nice shape, and her dimpled cheeks that were more pronounced when she smiled.

I moved over to her and told her to give me a few moments. Her body tensed when I went behind her. I imagined how she would have acted if I was a man. I ran my hands through her hair and made it into two cornrows. Her first look in the mirror I handed her made her gasp. It felt as though she had seen someone else.

From a box at the back of my shop, buried under a pile of papers, I pulled out a case of compact powder and shimmering lip balm.

More tears flowed, forming a path through her powdered face. Even before she said it, I knew that she hadn't ever paid this sort of attention to herself.

It was all we could do that day. But before she left, I told her the sort of clothes to wear and how to do the little things—wear a lip balm, smile, and pack your hair. "But most importantly, Mary. Never forget how beautiful you are." Both of her hands were in mine, her newly transformed face merely inches from mine. Gone was the look that she gave me when I had mentioned initially that all she needed was a belief in herself. I told her to practice everything for the next seven days and come back for the next session.

Two soft chimes pulled Ana from the world of the diary. A glance at her phone's screen revealed a text message from Theo.

"Want to meet up for drinks sometime soon?"

She marked the book and slid the pen between the diary pages before shutting it. She ran her hand over her face and let out another deep breath, this one deeper than the first. Her first instinct was to text "yes" and ask for time and place. But indecision froze her entire body. She couldn't even type "no."

She had been avoiding Theo for a reason. There was that deep attraction she felt for him, but there was no way she could tell him. She had done the best that she could do to keep it a secret from Andre. Telling Andre was the same as writing her feelings on her face and agreeing to go on a date with Theo. So, she ignored his jokes and told Andre that Theo was too young for her. But she knew it was all lies, and knowing Andre for whom he was, she could tell that he knew she was also lying.

The truth was that she was sexually attracted to him. Her nights have been filled with fantasies of him in her bed. Ana had never considered herself in such light—sexy, attractive. She had never told anyone, not even Andre, her best friend. What would she have told them anyways? That she didn't consider herself feminine enough to attract someone her age?

Flora would have snapped her fingers like someone that had just stumbled on an idea and replied, "I told you to spend time with people your own age. If you had, you wouldn't be thinking like this." Beneath those words would be the words she had always told her, "Settle down and get yourself a man."

She put her phone aside and made a mental note to reply to the message before the day was over. She needed to know how the next session between Gabriella and Mary turned out. That's another thing she noticed about Gabriella. It seemed as though she wrote the diary for someone.

The detail, the continuation of cases, made it all seem as though Gabriella had an inkling into whatever would happen to them much later. Ana grabbed the diary from her bedside stand, flipped it open, and her eyes fell to the page where she had previously stopped.

I noticed the difference even before she stepped in. Her expression was no longer vacant, her shoulders no longer stooped. The beauty that stood in the doorway surprised me. It has been barely two weeks since she had come to me for help. And she reminded me of something important— two weeks are enough, especially if the person takes all my counsel to heart.

Her question this time was, how could she draw her partner closer? "Closer?" I asked her, pretending not to understand what she meant.

We both burst into peals of laughter. "You want to have sex?" I asked. She smiled shyly, and a satisfying warmth filled my insides.

"Out of the many ways available for women to communicate their sexual desires to the men of their choice, I always settle for these two."

Mary leaned close; I could swear that she was my best student in that moment. Her body was balanced delicately at the edge of the chair.

"The first way is to say exactly what you want." Her face was a picture of alarm. Her eyes widened like eggs. I couldn't help but laugh. I reminded her that there was a reason I first taught her about building her self-esteem.

Women have to know that they have the same right as men to demand sex. I told her that subtlety was key, however. I understood her fears. We live in a world where a woman asking a man for sex could result in her being called many things. So, I told her that, provided she trusted her partner, she could start by telling him how much she is attracted to him and that she would love to experience sex with him.

The other way I told her is even more effective. It's called the showing rather than telling method. I waved away the fear that crept into her place. "Whenever you guys are in a private place. A place where you feel most comfortable. Show him that you desire him and also that you desire to share that experience with him. You could lean in for a kiss or rub your body against him. If he is ready, nothing will stop either of you. Men find a woman who takes what she wants extremely attractive."

As she left that day, I saw a mix of fear and confidence on her face. But I knew that she would be alright. She wasn't the first I had given those secrets to, and she certainly won't be the last.

●●●●●●●●

The food was extremely delicious. Shrimps with broccoli for her and scallops with mixed vegetables for Theo. The air around them was filled with scents that made them heady—roast chicken, fried rice, spiced vegetables. The air was filled with the noise of cutlery, the whisper of voices, and soft ambient music. But none of these prevented them from hearing each other.

Ana couldn't tell if it was because she hadn't seen him in a while or if it had always been like that; all she knew was that he looked so handsome that evening. It was the first thing she had told him.

His dark brown hair looked so in place, and she could tell that he had a haircut before he came. The white T-shirt that sat on his frame didn't just flatter his blue eyes; it also showed that he had been working out. She had almost gasped when she first saw him almost an hour ago. Matter of fact, an unfamiliar feeling of jealousy swept through her insides when she saw him in his white T-shirt paired with black jeans and matching boots. A leather jacket was slung on his arm and smile etched on his face. She wasn't the only one looking at him in that moment; she saw other girls also checking him out. She had shut her eyes and inhaled the scent of his perfume when they hugged, and just as she assumed, his hard body against hers confirmed that he had been spending some time in the gym. They had stayed that way for a long time, bodies pressed against each other, until a cleared throat behind them reminded them that they were standing in the doorway to the restaurant.

"Please tell me you like it," he said. He was wiping his bottom lip with one of the triangular folded napkins on the table. She had pointed to the stray sauce sliding down the corner of his pink lips moments before.

"I love it," she replied. But the food wasn't the only thing that she loved. She loved that she had been able to borrow a leaf from the diary and asked Theo to come home with her. She liked that he had agreed, and his enthusiasm had seemed as though he had been waiting for her to ask him over for months.

Much more than that, she liked that he noticed the new way that she styled her hair, the new coat of lipstick on her lips, and most importantly, the short floral dress that she paired with boots and a hat.

Gabriella would be proud of me, Ana thought.

"Sexy," that was the word he used, and there was no denying how much she loved the way his eyes sparkled and his lips curled when he said it.

They had talked about everything as though it was months, not weeks, that they had spent apart. Even from across the table, his hand had been reaching for hers. If he wasn't admiring her nails by running his finger over their tips, he was cradling her hands in his.

She would have reached across and practiced what Gabriella had told Mary in the diary, but she didn't want to push her luck. The restaurant, with its teeming crowd of the young and old, wasn't the place, and then wasn't the time. For her, the time was later.

Her mind traveled to her room. She had changed the sheets on her bed from the grey and white ones to new white ones. Afterward, she smoothed every wrinkle on the sheets till they were smooth as a pebble's surface. Her clothes had been folded neatly and put away in her closet. All her discarded shoes had been carefully arranged on her shoe rack. And even if the room looked spick and span, she still wasn't satisfied. It had taken her almost three days to reply to his messages, and the date was finally happening almost a week after his text.

As hard as it was, she had managed not to breathe a word of it to Andre. Even when she told him that she was leaving early that Friday. She had waved away his is-there-something-that-you-are-not-telling-me look. Her response was that she had to clean her room. She would tell him all the details on Monday, and as she thought about it, blood rushed to the surface of her skin.

•••••••

Ana's heart slammed hard against her chest as their lips met. Even moments before, she had doubted whatever she read in the diary. Telling Theo that she wanted to have sex with him was something that she couldn't do. No matter how much she tried. And she had tried. In the restaurant, as they were feeding themselves, in the cab on the way to her house. In her room as they both drank from the wine bottle. The words just wouldn't come out in the manner that she desired. But she discovered that showing would be better. She had prepared for the worst—him pushing her away or telling her that he wasn't ready.

But there was no pushing away, not even for a second. Instead, Theo's hands wrapped around her face as he kissed her back. Her room was cool, but she felt heat break out on her body as his lips hungrily traveled over hers.

She let her hand drop to his chest, and his also fell downward. Her body filled with sensations that she never knew she could possess.

It worked ... it works! Her mind screamed to no one in particular, and moments later, as their clothes were flying off, she reached beneath the diary and pulled out a packet of condoms. She was ready to go all the way.

12: BEGINNINGS AND ENDINGS

"Can you two keep your hands off each other?" Andre said in a voice that feigned seriousness. "At least until I'm out of the room," he added. His lips were pulled back in a smile, and his eyes brimming with the sort of happiness a parent watching their child take their first steps would have.

Ana rolled her eyes at him. Theo punched him playfully on his shoulder, but their hands remained linked to each other as they watched him attack his laptop keyboard. This sight pleased Ana a lot, seeing the two closest people in her life at ease with each other. She wondered how she would have felt if Theo and Andre didn't get along.

Their voices echoed around the room as though they were underwater.

Located in the basement of the building, the room reeked of old books, dust, and dampness. Flaking paint fell off in places, and there were boxes stacked everywhere. The only door leading to the room was a wooden monstrosity that creaked funnily when opened and felt heavy to the touch. A once-white fan with rusted blades adorned the still-white ceiling. Earlier, they had rid it of every bit of spiders and their webs. But a few could still be seen if the viewer paid keen attention.

They had dragged the large study table to the center. Every inch of it was filled with manuscripts and reams of unused papers stacked to a side. Three laptops were opened, and a printer that was once white was spewing more paper.

The diary was opened, and a blue pen lay comfortably in its center like a bookmark. Beside it were three notepads and two cell phones.

Three cups of coffee stood like sentries atop the papers, and a paper bag filled with untouched jam donuts rested on a pile of books. At the corner adjacent to the door was a wastebin basket half filled with balls of crumpled paper and packets of eaten food. Some of the papers that couldn't make it in lay on the floor beside it.

The room was well-lit by the two overhead light fixtures that made the white walls seem luminescent. An air conditioner system fed cool air into the room and made the summer heat bearable. Apart from the filled table, there was a single shelf lined with spiral-bound books and three chairs placed around the work table. Three jackets hung from the back of these chairs.

"I'm giving you this room because I trust both of you," Mr. Novak had said when he gave them the keys to one of the former library storerooms. The word "trust" coming from him had surprised Ana. Not that she had given him any reason to distrust her, but she never thought that Mr. Novak was the kind of person that would say something nice about anyone.

It had felt like a prank of some sort, and she had waited for him to call them back any moment and ask for the key. Later that day, she and Andre had talked about it. "I wouldn't have gone if you hadn't forced me to come along with you," She said, referring to Andre's insistence that they both went together to ask for a private space within the library where they could both work on the project.

"Are you sure that you are not jealous, Andre?" Ana replied finally. Her face has been as bright as dawn since she and Theo became official.

"Jealous?" Andre looked up from the laptop again. His large-framed glasses pushed up to the top of his head as he looked at the two lovebirds again. His forehead glistened with some of the gel from his well-slicked hair. This new hairstyle was one of the changes that had occurred in Andre's life, especially with the presence of his new boyfriend, Jack.

"Wait till you see me and Jack at the book launch," he teased. His hand was raised in the manner of someone taking an oath. Ana hadn't met him yet, but there was no doubt that whoever Jack was, he had come to stay in Andre's life.

"We will be the sweetest and the sexiest couple to ever walk this earth." He swung his shoulders as if sashing down the runway.

"So, help me God," Theo said as he detached his hand from Ana's and joined Andre in his fake-oath-declaration mode.

They all burst out laughing, the room echoing with their laughter.

It was hard to believe that, for the first time in her life, she had someone close to her that wasn't Andre. Someone close to her age. What was even more interesting was the fact that Theo was all hers. They had not put words to what they shared, but as Andre always teased her, Theo was her first serious boyfriend. This was a fact that he declared proudly because of his role in bringing them together.

She still couldn't forget the sounds that Andre had made in the library when she told him about her and Theo in her room. He had commented on how she glowed. Commenting on her lipstick and her choice of a dress instead of her typical T-shirt and jeans. She had finally let it slip.

His eyes had widened like orbs, his surprised gasps had felt as though he was choking, and for a moment, Ana thought he was. She ignored the heads that turned in their direction, although her eyes couldn't leave the entrance to Mr. Novak's office. It had become a habit, always looking out for him, always waiting for the appearance of his grumpy face.

Typical Andre, she mused as she rubbed his back. His gasps have transformed into hiccups.

She had planned to tell him during the break period. But the news in her chest felt like bubbles that couldn't hold still. So, she had broken her rule.

"Girl, I knew that you were up to something that Friday," he had said. His eyes were twinkling with excitement. They hadn't realized how much noise they were making until Mr. Novak appeared at his door. Ana's heart had plunged to her feet at the sight of his face. They were lucky he didn't see them. And as soon as his door closed, they both promised to continue from where they had stopped during the break period. As though they weren't the cause of the noise, they slipped into their roles and began patrolling the rows with stern faces.

At the cafeteria later that day, Ana dug into the sandwiches that Flora had made especially for her. It was then that she spilled all the details. She had even surprised herself with all the embellishments that she added. She had never been the kind of person to overstate facts or to blow things out of proportion. But she found it hard to describe the events of that evening without using superlatives or adding some extras to the story.

She told him that Flora had come down the stairs the next morning, just as she was seeing Theo out, and invited him for dinner with her parents.

He chanted "OMG" so long with his hands close to his mouth and his feet moving underneath him as though he was riding some invisible bicycle. Andre was the king of dramatic expressions, but she couldn't help laughing at his display.

The night with Theo had happened barely a week ago, but it seemed as though it was a lifetime ago. She had tried to dissuade Theo and Flora, but neither of them had agreed to rescind their decisions. And the thought of the dinner with Theo and her parents in a few hours still made her nervous.

"I think we had better get back to work," Ana said after she kissed Theo on the cheek.

"Sure, babe," Theo responded after placing a kiss on her forehead. Ana shot her tongue at Andre, whose head wagged at them in mock pity.

They both settled into the seats behind their computers and soon the room was filled with the sounds of clattering keyboards.

•••••••

Ana felt the knock on the door in her chest. Two sharp raps.

Even without seeing the person, she could tell that it was Theo.

She had learned in the few days since they had become an item how predictable he could be. His calls to her always came in at exactly 6:05 in the mornings, his afternoon texts at 12:00. And as she glanced at her watch, the hands pointed at exactly 4:00.

"Go and get the door for your boyfriend," Flora's shouted from the kitchen. Whatever response she had dried in her mouth when she saw the raised eyebrows on her mother's face.

The scent of fried, roasted, and baked food wafted into the air, making everyone's mouths water and their bellies grumble.

Even her mother, who was the less expressive of her parents, had remarked, "Flora, I think I'm going to have a double portion of whatever you are cooking today." Her father, on the other hand, had left them at the table to forage for whatever he could gobble in the kitchen.

Ana would have focused on the hunger if not for the rumbling in her chest. Theo joining her family for dinner made her a little nervous as well as a little proud.

The table was already brimming with casseroles and bottles of wine that her parents had brought back from Venice.

She stood unsteadily as the three pairs of eyes locked on her. Her legs felt like heavy weights as she made it to the door. She could hear the sound of her pounding heart and feel trickles of sweat running down her back.

"Her boyfriend is here," she heard Flora say in what was meant to be a whisper. Without even a word from her parents, she could feel their eyes drilling past her to the door in anticipation.

At least they will stop the chants of Venice, gondolas, and good times. Ana thought to herself.

Her parents had intentionally refused to talk about Theo. She knew why; they still believed that he wouldn't show, and from the way her mother, the most pessimistic of the pair, had cocked her head... He didn't exist.

The door seemed heavy as it slid on its hinges, but it was her heart that leaped to her mouth when she saw Theo at the door.

A picture of absolute perfection in a white shirt open at the neck underneath a brown leather jacket that matched his boots. His slightly tanned face glowed with health and reminded her of the sunny outdoors. She had to resist tucking the stray cowlick that fell across his eyes. His well-styled hair made him seem older than his age but in a very good way.

The scent of the roses in his hand wafted into her nostrils before her eyes settled on the bouquet. In his other hand, a bottle of wine wrapped in a brown paper bag sagged to his side. She hoped that he hadn't broken the bank to bring gifts.

The sound of more whispers and the scrapes of chairs behind her jolted her back to reality, and all she could pray for was that her parents would not embarrass her.

Before she realized what was happening, Theo leaned in and placed a wet kiss on her forehead. The spontaneity surprised her coming from someone who was as predictable as he was. The scent of his perfume found its way into her nostrils, and she felt like kissing him back. The memories of the last time he was there drifted temporarily into her mind.

Take it easy, Ana, she thought to herself.

Cold sweat broke out on the entire length of her body, and she couldn't help but exhale noisily as though she had just completed a race.

"Do you want to keep your guest at the doorway?" Flora's voice rang out behind her.

"Please come in," she managed to whisper.

•••••••

"Ana hasn't told us anything about you," her mother said in a voice that had a sing-song quality to it. She took a sip from her wine glass and wiped her lips with the folded napkin in front of her.

One thing Ana was sure about was that her mother liked Theo. Her mother wore her feelings on her sleeve.

"But you guys have not asked me about him," Ana wanted to say, but she decided against it. Things were going so well; she didn't want any awkwardness on her part to spoil it.

Ana looked from Theo's face to every other face at the table, and she realized in that moment that her mother wasn't the only one that liked him. Everyone did. Her father's face had fixed itself in a permanent smile since Theo came in. Flora's were even worse. She giggled at everything Theo said, even if it wasn't a joke. Perhaps she was excited that Ana finally had a boyfriend, or it was because Theo had told her that her meals were the best that he had ever tasted in his life. Ana couldn't tell.

Theo's face broke out in a smile of his own that seemed to suck all the air from the room. Her father had taken the words from her lips. Theo was indeed a wonderful charmer.

Folding his napkin in front of him, he told them about himself. His voice was clear and crisp, reminding her of one of the things that had drawn her to him. Most college students lacked the composure that he had. Those who had his composure couldn't speak as clearly as he could. And for a moment, a feeling of pride welled up in her chest.

She had thought that her parents would be taken aback because he was finishing up with college and still searching for work. But they weren't.

She thought about mentioning the project that they were all working on, but she decided to allow him to mention it himself. It would be rude to interrupt, and her parents didn't seem like they would pay any attention to her with the way they were gazing at Theo.

●●●●●●●●

The first time that she thought about it was the night she and Theo had sex. This was after the sounds of their moans and grunts had filled up the little space that was her room. A peculiar silence had eventually settled on the room like a blanket of some sort afterward. Exhausted and sticky, she had dragged herself to the bathroom.

It was in there that the thought had dropped as soon as the first droplets of water hit her body. She could remember how she had shivered at first at what seemed like the unusual coldness of the water. But the water had seemed normal later. Perhaps it was her body that was too hot. She thought. She couldn't tell which it was.

All she could remember was the droplets trailing down her body washing away sweat and other body fluids that had accumulated on her after the intense minutes within the sheets. Like ripples on the water's surface, tremors still ran through her body, making a simple task like sponging herself seem like an arduous task.

Ana had wished that Theo was there with her, just like she always saw in the movies. The couple showering together, and another round of sex occurring. But that was not to be.

Theo's naked body was splayed on the untidy and soiled bed sheets while their clothes and the thick comforter lay in a heap on the floor. Mingled with his soft snores was the voice of a pop star crooning about how he would make love to his new lover. The track had been on replay the way it had been since Theo had turned it on moments before they began. She could remember his eyes glazed with passion and his lips placed against her ears as he whispered, "So that Flora doesn't hear us." Not that Ana would have let anything stop her, Flora, or her parents. But she had nodded before meeting his lips with hers. These were the only sounds that punctured the silence that wrapped around them.

She couldn't tell exactly what brought the idea to mind. Perhaps it was the thought that Gabriella's formula had worked or the fact that Theo had told her that he was thinking of a topic to use for his final year project. Perhaps it was both. Even in this moment, she couldn't tell which of these was the trigger.

But she could remember leaping out of the bathroom, water dripping off her body like a wet dog that had just shaken itself vigorously. Her thick white towel wrapped around her body. Her eyes wide with excitement.

She had tapped Theo on his feet, eager to share the idea with him, to get a nod of approval from him or another angle to the thought. But he was fast asleep. His light snores only stopped for a brief moment before beginning again.

Not wanting to forget the idea, she reached for her notepad and a pencil. Less than a minute later, she filled the page with the idea. It sounded ridiculous, impossible to achieve even, and she thought more than once to rip the page and dump it into the almost full waste bin beside the bathroom door.

The next morning before she snuck Theo out of the house, she said, "I'm going to adapt the diary into a non-fiction novel." She was full of excitement that was bubbling within her like the fizz of an effervescent drink. His eyes were blank at first; to him, she seemed like someone teetering at the edge of insanity. He had held her hand in one of his, while with the other, he had held her chin in place.

"What diary? What book?" he asked her. His face still bearing the telltale signs of a long sleep, his brows furrowed in confusion.

"Gabriella's diary," she answered. Her voice louder than she had intended it to be. Andre's confusion wasn't any different. His was even worse. He had erupted into loud laughter. The kind that would have put them in trouble if they weren't in the cafeteria.

"You can't be serious," he finally said. His hands had dropped to his lap. Because her face had remained serious and resolute, he looked at her with his serious face and a look of understanding.

The next day, they began planning. He asked her all the questions, she provided all the answers. Soon, their notepads were filled with plans and more plans. Soon, Andre was the one that began setting timelines and targets, action plans, and goals.

He was the one who suggested that they ask for a room in the library where they could write and edit. She was the one who reached out to the half-dozen publishing agencies on Instagram that all turned them down. It was Theo that suggested that they spend one hour in the morning before work and two hours after work to work on the book. He was even the one that suggested the book title that she finally settled on. *The Catalogues of Desire and Disappearance: A true life story.*

These were the thoughts that traversed Ana's mind as she sat at the table flanked by Theo and Andre for the book signing. The pile of books formed a tower of sorts beside her, the line of excited fans smiling and sliding their purchased copies for her signature increased in front of her. Signage with her face and the book lined the way from the gate to the entrance and every vantage point in the hall.

I must be dreaming… this cannot be real, Ana thought.

It still felt unreal, as though she was having an out-of-body experience of some sort. The success of the book had come like a flood, too fast and too much. And on some mornings, she still woke up to ask herself if her life was a dream or reality.

The publishing company had paid her an advance, even before the first copy was printed. Offers were pouring in for a movie adaptation, and her entire month was planned for interviews and visits to bookstores.

Just then, Theo slid a slip of paper to her, and when she looked at it, she could only shiver.

You are up for a speech in five minutes.

EPILOGUE

She had already marked it for deletion when she saw it in the pile of messages marked for deletion. Whoever had sent it had meant for her to see it, especially with the title of the email and the way it was written in block letters. It could not be missed. It felt like a beacon at sea, like a waving flag of some sort.

THE STORY NEVER ENDED

Ana hesitated before she clicked on it since her life, indeed all their lives, had changed. She had had to surf through piles of mail and hundreds of emails. Most of the emails were fan emails from the LGBTQ+ community, while others were offers from publishers across the globe who wanted to publish the book in other languages apart from German. She now had a lawyer, and she had spoken to publishers in countries as far away as Egypt and Kazakhstan.

The rest of the emails were from people who claimed to be friends or relatives.

And to declutter her inbox, she had ensured that at the end of every day, all unread and unnecessary emails were deleted and flushed away to the email graveyard.

Her eyes were heavy with exhaustion. Her bones hurt like hell. If anyone had asked her what she wanted, she would have answered in one word—sleep. The day had gone the same way that their days now went—busy.

Half of it was spent on the road, the other part was spent sitting, smiling, and signing. Even though it wasn't ever tiring signing copies of the book, posing for pictures with fans, and answering questions from journalists, they always had to pay the price at night. They had all talked about it, and the experience had been the same for all of them.

No one had told them that celebrity status came with its stress. And as they learned it, they all confessed that they would have preferred their former lives to this. But they all knew that whatever was left of their former lives was gone with the wind. So, she decided to read just a few lines and delete the message if it did not make any sense. With her decision made, she slid on her reading glasses, leaned back into the headboard, and clicked on the email.

Dear Ana,

I hope that you finally get to see this email. I really do. I can only imagine the number of emails that you get daily or the letters that come in the mail. I know this because I have sent several myself, and not one was replied to. I tried this as the last resort. Some of the kids here claim that it's easier to send emails and that they are faster to deliver also.

I know that you might be wondering who wrote you. You will soon find out. It is hard to shield myself from someone who has had a peep into parts of my life.

I have always known about the power of stories and how they can connect perfect strangers together. But I didn't really know how powerful they really were until I heard the lady reporter on the television talk about the book. I am also aware of the buzz that the book has created. Tears had streamed down my face the day I read it. Even with the name change, I can tell that it was my story, our story, that was told. People only forget the things that do not matter to them. All that happened, the ones that you were able to capture, mattered to me, and they still do.

Ana adjusted herself on the bed. The new bed didn't creak under her weight. It was one of the changes that had occurred in her life. Sometimes when the thought crossed her mind, she wondered why she had changed it since she would be moving out of Flora's place soon. The presence of Theo in her life and her new status seemed to relax her parents' stance on her.

But as always, she had waved the thought away like she found herself doing recently. Andre's voice drifted to her ears, "It's a celebrity thing, right?" Her face lit up with a smile.

She felt like stopping and just forwarding the email to Andre and Theo and ask that they all check it out together in the morning. And she would have until her eyes fell on the next line.

The story didn't end where your book ended. It wasn't an end; it was a beginning.

Ana felt her heart pound. It almost felt as though someone was in the room with her. The sensation of being watched crawled over her skin. The laptop suddenly felt heavy on her legs, and it almost tipped over. Even the air felt warm and heavy. Only the familiarity of her environment reassured her—the white board of her wardrobe, her tiny bookcase that held about twenty books, her coat hanger, and the sight of her discarded shoes. These were the familiar sights that reassured her.

"Impossible," she muttered. Her free hands slammed against the bed while the other held the laptop in place. "Gabriella and Bernd are dead," she said aloud, this time as though she was speaking to an audience. Her hand fell to her bedside drawer, hoping to find the diary there. The empty surface reminded her that the diary was now in safe keep in the special section of the library. She returned her attention to the screen.

It's so exciting that our dreams finally came true many decades after we were hounded like wild animals for daring to live the truth of ourselves. I am close to tears as I write this message to you. You may not even understand how life in the 1980s was in East Germany. The diary couldn't capture it all, neither could the letters.

Today, I hear that from the comfort of my living room, anyone could shop for and indeed buy any of the sex toys that I had to sell in secret. I have even been told that people could get any of the tips and lessons with just a flick of their phone's buttons or a click of a mouse. So easy. So harmless. So unreal.

Nowadays, I see queer couples kiss on the street, pride parades held in a city where our friends were once captured and taken away forever. I'm filled with a mix of happiness and sadness. It is more happiness than sadness now. Bernd is now free to cross-dress as he loves. He tells me that he has never felt happier than in this moment. We are now a trouple. Isn't that what you guys now call three people in a relationship. Xavi is the third partner in our relationship. He was the one who helped us move to Spain back in those days when our only prayer was to see a new day.

He used to be one of Bernd's partners, one of the people that attended the parties I always had back then. It is true what they say. One good turn always begets another.

We live together on a farm near Barcelona. And one of these days, we hope to visit Germany. I know that you might want to know if I still give advice to couples or if we still have those parties that you described in your book. The answer is no. We spend our days as a happy family, living, loving, and laughing. The world has changed since when we left East Berlin. No one from our past knows about us. And no one in our present knows about that part of my past. Spain is different from Germany. At the least, the part of Barcelona that we live in is. I never thought that this time would come. A time when I will have the chance to say thank you to someone who was courageous enough to tell a story that we never thought we would be able to tell. But here I am, and I am hoping that this medium will be able to do justice to that.

As I said, our stories didn't end in those nameless hotels or on the run from the agents of the communist police. Even after all those years, we still wake up with our bodies covered in cold sweat and our hearts slamming in our chests as the memories of the past slip into our present. But no doubt it is all better now. And we are grateful that we survived to live in a world where people could live, in a world as free as this.

It was when the first tear drops hit the surface of her keyboard that Ana realized that she had been crying.

Printed in Great Britain
by Amazon